"I think [...] about o[...] relationship."

Sunny spoke whimsically and reached out an inviting hand. "I have a vision.... I'm going to knock this all down. First the fence, then the house."

Jackie glared at him. "This is my home. I'd never permit it."

His eyes laughed at her. "That's what I was told before I made *Eye for an Eye*. Impossible. But I did it. Our children—"

"You haven't got any children."

"That's why we have to get started as soon as possible."

"You don't even know me," Jackie shrilled. "And I don't like you."

"Take the grand approach to life," he said reproachfully. "You know you want me. We'd make a great couple."

For some unaccountable reason Jackie's heart was leaping. "Are you actually proposing to me?"

EMMA DARCY nearly became an actress until her fiancé declared he preferred to attend the theatre *with* her. She became a wife and mother. Later she took up oil painting—unsuccessfully, she remarks. Then, she tried architecture, designing the family home in New South Wales. Next came romance writing—"the hardest and most challenging of all the activities," she confesses.

Books by Emma Darcy

HARLEQUIN PRESENTS

EMMA DARCY

strike at the heart

Harlequin Books

TORONTO • NEW YORK • LONDON
AMSTERDAM • PARIS • SYDNEY • HAMBURG
STOCKHOLM • ATHENS • TOKYO • MILAN

For Taurus with Leo rising—
who inspired this book and has struck
at the heart of all we have written—
a small token of our admiration and gratitude

Harlequin Presents first edition February 1988
ISBN 0-373-11048-0

Original hardcover edition published in 1987
by Mills & Boon Limited

CHAPTER ONE

NOISE pollution! That's what it was. A crude, barbaric crime against the peace and quiet of the countryside. But of course Sunny King knew there was no police station within easy reach. He knew it was perfectly safe for him to carry on any sort of depraved orgy for as long as he liked, without any consideration to bird or beast or person unfortunate enough to be his neighbour. That was undoubtedly why he had come to St Alban's, surrounding himself with enough property to ensure privacy. It was a malicious trick of fate that he had chosen to buy the property next to hers.

If only it wasn't so damned hot! On a cooler night she could have shut the doors and windows, blocking out the nerve-jangling volume of sound. But no! He had to pick the hottest night of the year to have his rotten house-warming party. It probably suited him. All his fancy guests were undoubtedly prancing naked to the primitive beat of that rock band. They would have to be drunk or drugged to stand the noise. Every amplifier the band had was turned up to maximum output. Jackie wondered how one went about acquiring a plastic bomb.

Her house was like a baker's oven: airless, stifling, oppressive. She could feel perspiration trickling down her back; the light cotton nightie was sticking to her in places. How the boys had been able to sleep in this heat, with that racket going on, was almost incredible, but there'd been no sound from them since she'd ordered them to bed.

Here she was, virtually stewing in her own juices, no closer to sleep than she had been two hours ago. And it was now past one in the morning. For how much longer was that heavy rock music going to blare? Probably until dawn, she decided, kicking irritably at the hot sheets.

In a burst of frustration Jackie rolled off the bed, stomped out to the veranda and glared across at Sunny King's property. Sunny King! What a ridiculous name for a man! Yet it suited the egocentric, show-off type of person he was. And what else could be expected of the latest shining star in the movie world?

The most successful producer/director of films in Australia, the local newspaper had proclaimed when he had favoured St Alban's by choosing to live in the area. The article had been most effusive about his marvellous career, but in actual fact he had only hit the big-time with his last two movies. Apparently blood-curdling violence was big box office, and Sunny King had capitalised on it by creating a cult-figure hero who went about slaughtering enemies like a killing machine.

It disgusted Jackie that such a hero could have so much popular appeal. Even her own sons thought the one-eyed avenger, Dirk Vescum, was terrific. It disgusted her even further that Sunny King had got rich by tapping the baser instincts in people. And right now she felt a monumental disgust that she had to put up with his living next door to her.

He was supposed to have come here because the relative isolation of the countryside would give him the peace and quiet necessary to work on ideas for his movies. Peace and quiet! She wished she could give him peace and quiet all right. In a padded cell!

Only a madman could have built such a monstrosity of a house. He even had the arrogance to call it King's Folly. With all its stupid turrets it was more like Court Jester's Folly. The man had no sensitivity towards the environment, no sensitivity at all.

Jackie's mouth curled in disdain at Sunny King and all he stood for. These newly rich people despoiled everything they touched. They had no manners, no civility, no sophistication. He had not even had the courtesy to return her neighbourly call. Admittedly only his secretary, Trevor Haines, had been in residence at the time, but he had said he would pass on her greetings.

But the great Sunny King hadn't bothered to introduce himself to his next-door neighbour. Nor invite her and the children to his house-warming party. Not that she would have gone, but he could have given her the pleasure of refusing his invitation. The man was crass!

It was a terrible shame to see the way the whole district was losing its identity. The old families were dying off or selling out, and the newcomers had no real respect for the land and its traditions. All they wanted was the luxury of hectares of land around their ostentatious homes. The history of the settlement of the Macdonald's River and the village of St Alban's meant little or nothing to them. They had swooped in because of the far more attractive asset of being within easy commuting distance to Sydney.

Jackie heaved a resentful sigh and turned her back on the offensive sight and sound of Sunny King's party. She wandered restlessly along the veranda which ran around three sides of her small weatherboard house. There was a waft of breeze coming from the south. If she dragged the spare mattress out on to the veranda, she might get some sleep.

Ten minutes later she had managed to pull the bedding through the front doorway and was comfortably settled on it. Even her pillow felt cooler. There was definitely a light breeze coming over the front steps. She stuffed wadded cotton-wool into her ears, which diminished the noise considerably, and it wasn't long before she drifted off to sleep.

The light pressure on her mouth and the slight tickle of Geoff's beard on her chin gradually lifted her out of deep sleep and into dreamy contentment. She lifted an arm and curled it around his neck and her lips parted on a sigh of drowsy pleasure, inviting another kiss. His tongue tingled over the inner side of her lips and she met it with her own, teasing back as she langourousely moved her body towards his. The pleasantly erotic play of the kiss quickly deepened, jolting her fully awake with its passionate demand.

But it wasn't Geoff kissing her! He had never kissed her like this; and Geoff was dead, dead and buried four years ago! Jackie opened her eyes, shocked out of her wits. She saw a mane of golden hair shining above her in the moonlight. Fear paralysed her into rigidity. She had read about rape but had never expected to experience it. And she couldn't even scream! That cursedly persuasive mouth was plundering hers with mounting intensity.

He had moved the top half of his body over hers, pinning one of her arms underneath him, but the one she had curled around his neck was free. She raked her fingernails down his back. She found it was strong and muscular, and he only seemed to take encouragement from the action. She kicked out with both legs. They hit nothing.

Panic drove her hand back up into his thick hair and her fingers tugged fiercely at it. The pressure on her mouth relaxed. The man slowly lifted his head, a deep sigh whispering from his still-parted lips; full, sensual lips, she noted resentfully. She could smell the alcohol on his breath. She didn't know the man. She had never seen anyone remotely like him in her entire life.

It was the beard that had fooled her in that moment between sleep and wakefulness, but it was unlike Geoff's beard. It was golden for a start, and barbered to an aggressive point. Even his eyebrows were golden, glistening above eyes that were twinkling with devilish mischief. Which suggested he couldn't be a serious rapist.

Jackie activated her vocal chords, even though they felt positively strangled. 'Who ... who are you?'

The full lips curved whimsically as he stroked her cheek with featherlight fingertips. 'How very beautiful you are.' His voice was a soft musical croon, as enchanting as a sigh of wind through a grove of trees.

For one wildly imaginative moment Jackie fancied him as a Norse god, straight out of the myths and legends, but common sense and the reality of firm, warm flesh and blood pressing against her chest quickly dispelled that romantic notion. 'You ... you get away from me,' she snarled at him. 'Leave me alone.'

The smile widened to a gleam of white teeth. 'When you speak with so much repressed feeling, your breasts rise and gently caress my chest. Do you realise how exciting that is?'

She suddenly realised his chest was bare. And she had raked bare skin on his back. My God! Was he completely naked? 'You get off me this instant,' she squeaked, then swiftly drew breath for more vehemence. 'If you don't get off me I'll call my husband and he'll shoot you. Both barrels of a twelve-gauge shotgun.'

His soft chuckle was a musical mockery of her threat. 'Mrs Mulholland, your husband died four years ago, climbing the north face of the Matterhorn. From exposure, I believe. I also know that you're completely alone here and at my mercy,' he added teasingly.

Her thoughts winged instantly to the boys, innocently asleep at the back of the house. But she could not call out to them. She could not risk involving them if there was any danger. 'How do you know that?' she prevaricated.

'I have my sources of information,' was the blithe reply.

'Who are you?' she asked again, more insistently.

He dragged himself off her with a reluctant sigh.

Jackie scrambled to her feet and was up, her back pressed against the door-jamb in protective readiness, before he straightened to his full height, which was far too impressive for her peace of mind. The swimming trunks he wore—if that was what they were—barely covered his private parts, and the body on show was an artist's dream: a flowing line of firm flesh and muscle in perfect proportion.

He nonchalantly leaned back against the veranda railing and grinned at her. 'No cause for fight or flight. You've just had the pleasure of meeting Sunny King.'

The arrogance of the man! The sheer, blazing arrogance! Not to mention... Jackie's voice dripped ice. 'It wasn't a pleasure, Mr King. It was ...' Her mind whizzed through its stored vocabulary for a suitable put-down and she produced it with venom. '... disgusting!' Her voice rose in outrage. 'How dare you do that to me?'

He looked pained and his hand waved an appeasing gesture. 'Mrs Mulholland, you simply misread the situation. I was only practising a device I learnt on safari in South Africa. Best way of waking someone up without frightening them. Always used it on the women when lions and tigers were on the prowl.'

'Not to mention yourself, Mr King,' she snapped contemptuously. 'Don't try to sweet-talk me. I ...'

'Please call me Sunny.'

'I know precisely who you are and all you've done. I've even seen a couple of the early movies you produced ...'

'Marvellous!'

'... all of which were crummy!' Jackie topped him with triumphant satisfaction. 'Just because you got lucky and made a cult movie on a shoestring budget ...'

He held up his palm. 'Say no more. I understand everything. You resent my success.'

Jackie snarled at his smug visage. '... don't think you can steal up on me in the middle of the night and start kissing me. Now, get the hell off my place!'

He folded his arms and nodded gravely. 'Certainly. Never stay where I'm not wanted. Sorry you don't want to be neighbourly. What do you want me to do with the boys?'

Jackie's outrage blanked into confusion. 'What boys?' Surely to God they were safely asleep in bed! There hadn't been a squeak out of either of them.

The smile on Sunny King's face was one of pleasant indifference. 'Let me see now,' he drawled. 'There's the one called Robert Falcon, after the Scott who explored the Antarctic, and the other called Edmund Percival, after the Hillary who climbed to the top of Mount Everest.'

Every maternal hackle in Jackie's body rose to the fore. 'Where are my children?' she demanded fiercely.

'We discovered them up a tree, observing our party at close range. At the present moment they are discussing abseiling with my secretary, Trevor Haines. They didn't seem terribly eager to leave, so I took it upon myself, out of the kindness of my heart, to ...'

'I'm sorry you've been troubled with them,'

Jackie cut in stiffly. 'I'll come and bring them home.'

'No trouble. No trouble at all. Terribly fortunate. If I hadn't thought you might be worried by their absence if you happened to discover it, I wouldn't have come down. And here you were, lying in the moonlight, a picture of beauty revealed . . .'

A flood of heat ripped through Jackie's body as she remembered just how thin her cotton nightie was. 'I'll go and get dressed straight away,' she gabbled and darted into the darkness of the hallway.

'No hurry,' floated after her. 'The night is still young, the air scented with magic, the . . .'

Those damned little monkeys, Jackie seethed, throwing open their bedroom door to check that their beds were indeed empty. Which they were. And the window wide open. Just wait until she got her hands on them!

She banged into the bathroom, slapped some water on her face, and pulled a brush through her short black hair. Beauty revealed, she scoffed at herself in the mirror. Well, she supposed she didn't look too bad for a thirty-one-year-old. Her skin was still creamy smooth and her thick-lashed eyes were as good as they had always been. A tantalising hazel, Geoff used to say. And her . . . Oh, good God! What on earth was she doing, taking notice of that stupid Sunny King? She wrinkled her dainty little nose in disgust and stomped into her bedroom.

Those disobedient little brats were going to get the tongue-lashing of their lives. Here it was—she glanced at the bedside clock—almost two in the morning, and she had to trek up to that den of iniquity to collect them. And what the devil would she put on?

She threw off her nightie, grabbed a pair of briefs from her underwear drawer and dragged them on, then turned to the wardrobe, deciding any old dress would do. She was certainly not going partying at Sunny King's place.

'You know, for a woman who's had two kids, you have a fantastic body.'

She whipped around to find Sunny King propped indolently against the door-jamb, eyeing her with unashamed lechery.

'Luscious breasts. Just right,' he observed appreciatively.

Fire burned into her cheeks as temper soared to boiling point. 'You really are the end!' she snapped at him, whipping out a top and dragging it over her torso.

'I bet you'd win any wet T-shirt competition you went in,' he mused.

'Will you get out of here?' she yelled, snatching up the shorts she had let drop on to the floor last night.

'I'm patiently waiting for you. Got the car outside ready to run you down the road. I do like short shorts, particularly on a cheeky bottom.'

'Do you make a profession of being offensive?' she grated at him, slipping her feet into a pair of sandals.

'Me? Offensive?' The golden eyebrows rose into surprised peaks but his eyes were laughing at her.

Blue eyes, she noticed. Bedroom eyes, she thought as she scorned his profession of innocence. 'Assaulting defenceless women. Voyeurism. No respect for privacy ...'

'Do you begrudge me a few primitive urges?' he cut in with teasing mockery. 'That's the trouble with today's society. Too uptight. Lost touch with their basic selves. Let it all flow out, I say.'

'Well, if you don't mind, I'd like to flow down the road and collect my children,' Jackie shot at him with acid sarcasm.

His arm swept an invitation. 'At your service.'

He did not move and she was forced to brush past him. He had the gall to pat her bottom and Jackie fumed with frustration. Male chauvinist pig! Her hand itched to belt his insolent face but common sense told her that discretion was the better part of valour.

Better to get him back to his party for his fun and games; any tussle with him here could only lead to further indignities. But next time she would be ready for him, with the twelve-gauge shotgun on hand. If there ever was a next time, and please God there wouldn't be! Sunny King would never set foot on her place again if she could help it.

A long sleek sports car stood at the gate. It glinted golden, too. Just who did he think he was? The Sun-king? Had he coined his ridiculous name from the God of ancient Egypt? He was so damned full of himself.

'It's a Lagonda,' he said proudly as he opened the passenger door for her.

The car screamed wealth, luxury and performance, and once Sunny King took the wheel, he let it perform. The tyres screeched as he slammed his foot on the accelerator. Jackie sagged back in the seat. Show-off, she notched up silently. It went neatly with all his other faults.

They screamed down the road. Braking heavily, Sunny King slid the car sideways to line it up with his own driveway. Then once again the fierce acceleration as he zoomed up to the house, spraying gravel everywhere with an abrupt halt in front of the triple garage.

'Nice car,' he said with a wide smile, patting the wheel benevolently as he added, 'worth about twice the price of a Rolls.'

Jackie added boastfulness to the list of vices. 'Thanks for the lift,' she said sarcastically. 'I'll get the children out of your hair and be on my way.'

'I'll drive you back.'

Jackie gritted her teeth into a semblance of a smile. 'No. Please don't do that.' Once was quite enough. She was lucky to have arrived safely and she wasn't going to risk a return trip. 'We'll walk,' she said firmly.

'Nonsense. Besides, I want you to stay a while. You haven't seen through the house and it'll give me great pleasure to show it to you. I'm very proud of it.'

Jackie added pride to the list. In an effort to be fair, she wondered if he had any virtues at all, but a moment's recollection brought none to mind. She suffered the light grasp on her arm as he led her to the house.

'It's very late,' she stated firmly.

He grinned at her, completely irrepressible. 'Just a few minutes of your time to dwell on one of the new wonders of the world.'

He threw open the double front doors. Just inside, flanking the entrance, stood two statues, copies of Greek sculpture, both nude figures. If that was not enough, the sounds of uninhibited revelry rooted Jackie's feet to the ground. Fortunately the rock band had taken a break so her voice was clearly audible as she laid down the line.

'It is late, Mr King. My children should have been in bed hours ago. I do not wish to come in. If you would please see that the boys are brought to me, we will not delay you from your guests any longer.'

He eyed the mutinous set of her face, adopted a crestfallen look for a moment, and, when that had no softening effect on her expression, shrugged his shoulders and stepped over to the balustrade which separated the mezzanine foyer from the floor below. 'Trevor!' he roared at the top of his voice.

There was a chorus of welcoming cries.

'Hey, Sunny!'

'Where've you been, man?'

'Come on down and join the party!'

Jackie watched sourly as he waved a kingly salute.

His secretary came bounding up the curved staircase on the right. He was a young man, full of bright enthusiasm, eager to carry out any of his employer's whims. Jackie eyed him with increasing jaundice. Obviously a born yes-man. He gave the impression of worshipping the ground on which Sunny King walked.

'What have you done with Robert and Edmund?' the great man asked.

Jackie approved of that direct question.

Trevor Haines caught sight of her. 'Oh, Mrs Mulholland. It's all right. They're here somewhere.'

'Trevor, how come you know Mrs Mulholland?' Sunny demanded a little peevishly.

'I told you that Mrs Mulholland had called by, Sunny. Remember? And you said ...'

He waved a dismissive hand. 'You neglected to mention she was a beautiful young widow,' he said accusingly. 'You did wrong.'

'Well, I ...' His young face went a bright beet-root red as he turned to Jackie in apology.

She had to choke back a laugh. To Trevor, who was only in his early twenties, she was not young, and what beauty she had was only in the eye of the beholder. But they were straying from the business in hand. 'The boys?' she reminded him.

'Oh, they are here, Mrs Mulholland,' he quickly assured her. 'I had to deal with ... uh ... some other business, and they asked if they could look through the house, and I knew Sunny wouldn't mind, so I told them to go ahead.'

'Splendid!' his employer declared, clapping him on the back with approval. 'Nothing for you to worry about, Trevor. Mrs Mulholland and I will go and find them.' And he turned to her with smug triumph written all over his face.

So there was to be no avoiding entering the lion's den. But let him try anything! Just let him try anything more on her and he would see who had claws!

CHAPTER TWO

MAKING movies had obviously gone to Sunny King's head in a big way, Jackie decided. And so had the money he had made. The entrance to his home reminded her of the balcony at the State Theatre. Mottled Greek columns lined the staircase which curved downwards from either side of the foyer; little alcoves in the wall held more statues, all of them nude; huge chandeliers hung from the enormously tall ceiling. Pompous and pretentious. No other words for it.

As they started the descent—to the pits, Jackie privately labelled the huge entertainment-room below—Sunny King hung a hand on her shoulder and grinned down at her. 'Fit for a king, isn't it?' The pun on his own name obviously gave him a lot of satisfaction.

Jackie dropped her shoulder and stepped sideways, giving him her best look of disdain. 'It reeks of wealth, if that's any commendation.'

He chuckled, his twinkling blue gaze skating over the prominent outline of her breasts. 'True. But it has given me enormous pleasure to create one of the majestic homes of the century. The great movie actresses of the past would have given their eye-teeth to make a dramatic entrance down these steps.'

Jackie's mouth clamped into a thin line. There was no point in rising to his grandiose spiel. Clearly his hide was so thick it couldn't be punctured, no matter what she said.

'Come and I'll introduce you to some of today's stars,' he continued with unflagging enthusiasm, his hand making its way around her waist this time. 'Most of the cast from ...'

She stopped dead. 'Mr King, I am not here to play the star-struck fan. I am here to take my children home.' She waved a dismissive hand at the crowd of guests below them. 'I don't see them down there. Do you?'

He didn't bother to look. His gaze was fixed on her uptilted face. 'Do you know there are gold flecks in your eyes? Gives them a tigerish quality. I bet you'll love the guest-room in the turret. It's just through here.'

He steered her into a passageway off the first landing and opened a door, virtually bundling her inside the room as he switched on the light. Jackie's eyes almost rolled in their sockets at the incredible décor. It was some mad cross between a sheikh's tent and a safari nightmare. Great loops of tiger-printed material fell from a high central peak, which she imagined reached to the ceiling, and draped the whole of the circular wall. The quilt on the bed featured quilted tigers and the floor had tiger-skin rugs all over it.

'What do you think?' Sunny King asked with all the eagerness of a little boy who wanted to be patted on the head.

Jackie was struck dumb.

'Knocked you speechless?' he crowed. 'Wait till you see the rest.'

Never, not in magazines, in movies, in any crazy stretch of the imagination, had Jackie seen such rampant opulence as Sunny King showed her in his guided tour. The dining-room was all blue and gold—peacock-blue with decorative jars of peacock feathers, which was certainly in character for her host. The private movie theatre was all plush red—naturally. The kitchen was surely the largest in the world and equipped with every gadget under the sun. Jackie had hoped to find the boys there, feeding their faces or guzzling free soft drink, but so such luck.

Beyond the central entertainment-room, which ended in a spectacular wall of glass, was a flagstoned terrace of tennis-court proportions, and Jackie noted that the rock band was set up out there, which explained why the music had been so loud. She winced as she saw the band members picking up their instruments once more. There were people everywhere but still no sign of Robert and Edmund. She wondered if they had sneaked back home in an attempt to avoid trouble.

Sunny King kept urging her around his dazzling domain: the games-room with its lush billiard table, mirrored bar and sunken swimming-pool; mind-boggling bathrooms with spas and saunas; bedrooms galore, each one a master-piece of vulgar sensuality where the furnishings were concerned. There was no doubt about it, the man was nothing but a satyr.

'And finally we come to the *pièce de résistance*, the master bedroom,' Sunny King purred in her ear, and opened the door with a flourish.

Jackie came to an abrupt halt in the doorway. Her eyes glazed as they took in the massive four-poster bed with its golden gauze curtaining. The walls featured the more pornographic paintings of Norman Lindsay. The ceiling was painted like the Sistine Chapel, except the theme was certainly not heavenly.

'Wish I could have got Michelangelo to do that, but apparently he's dead,' Sunny King said with a cheerfully lascivious grin. 'However, the carving on the bedhead is marvellous. Inspirational. It came from Bali.'

He moved across the room to sweep the nearest curtain aside. He waved an invitation to her. 'Have a look! It's incredibly clever how everything intertwines. Master craftsmen.'

Jackie could imagine what was intertwined and she wasn't budging a foot inside this sybarite's bedroom.

'Don't be shy,' he urged. 'You'll like it.'

She had seen more than enough and the boys had obviously skipped out somewhere along the line. 'Do you really want my opinion, Mr King?' she asked silkily.

'Sunny,' he corrected her with a confident smile. 'And yes, I would like your opinion.'

'I think it's dreadful,' she said with lofty disdain.

The smile faltered and slowly curled into something else as he strolled back to her. 'So I can't impress you, Mrs Mulholland?'

She sensed danger but recklessly defied it. 'Not a ghost of a chance, Mr King.'

'Is that right? Then you shouldn't be standing under the mistletoe.'

Jackie glanced up in disbelief and that momentary reaction was her undoing. Before she could strike a defensive stance, Sunny King was holding her and kissing her again. She tried to struggle against his embrace but that didn't work. His arms were too strong and he moved in closer, his thighs pressing against hers. Not just pressing but rubbing in a sensual manner that made her electrically aware of the silken down on his legs. For one awful moment she felt her own thighs quiver in . . . in pleasure?

Alarm bells went off in Jackie's head. Passive resistance had to be employed. Sunny King's mountainous ego wouldn't like that and he would soon get tired of trying to wring blood out of a stone. Be as still and as cold as his damned statues, she told herself. A few moments were enough to convince her that passive resistance didn't work.

His mouth played over hers with tantalising persuasiveness, and he took advantage of the lack of resistance to slide his hands down the curve of her spine and curl them around her bottom. His body swayed erotically against hers. No crude thrusting. Oh no! A provocative teasing that built anticipation to an explosive need to clutch him to her, hold him fast, grind her own body into his.

Her whole nervous system was going haywire, sending a chaotic mass of urgent messages to her brain. Melt! Give in! Take him! Forget everything else! Only this matters now! Now, now, now!

Sanity fought back. Sunny King was a vain, proud prig of a man who thought he could sweep her off her feet, and was obviously intent on doing so. He had arrogantly taken advantage of her, as he undoubtedly did with any woman who crossed his lecherous path. To let him have her as another conquest was unthinkable. Totally unacceptable.

But it had been so long since she had been aroused like this, so long since such excitement had been swarming through her veins ... her whole body pulsing with ...

Jackie ruthlessly crushed the treacherous wail of thought. Not Sunny King, pride insisted. Never him! She slid her hands up to his shoulders, meaning to lever herself away. He chose that moment to clamp her lower body to his and all stomach for resistance collapsed. She gasped as desire shot through her in a gathering spiral of heat that plastered her to him in weak abandonment. His mouth seduced hers with an erotic invasion that scrambled any possibility of rational thought. She responded with wild, mindless passion.

Some four metres away, underneath the king-size four-poster bed, Edmund wriggled over to Robert and tapped his shoulder. 'Do you think they're gone?' he whispered.

Robert frowned his uncertainty. 'Don't know.'

Edmund rolled his eyes. 'We're going to cop it. That was Mum and she didn't sound happy.'

'She's mad as hell, I reckon.'

There was a moment of mournful silence while they contemplated their prospective fates. 'It was worth it anyway,' Robert decided.

'Yeah,' his younger brother agreed. Edmund's persistently inquisitive mind pulled out a curious remark. 'I didn't see any mistletoe.'

'Me neither. I'm going to take a peek.'

With all the guile of twelve-year-old deviousness, he slithered to the corner of the bed where the gold brocade valance was slit to fit around the corner-post. With his face pressed hard to the carpet he lifted the flap far enough to get a sight of the floor between him and the doorway. The vision of two pairs of feet toe to toe, one set of which were encased in his mother's sandals, absolutely intrigued him. He poked his head out a little further. Edmund wriggled up beside him to see for himself. They looked at one another in startled wonder and ducked back behind the valance.

'Mum's kissing Sunny King!' Edmund's whispered voice carried a peculiar note of awe.

'They're just about glued together,' Robert agreed, even more awed.

Caution was swept aside by a novelty too great to be missed. Both heads poked out from under the bed, eyes agog with fascinated interest.

Sunny King chose that particular moment to

lift Jackie off her feet—only far enough to serve the dual purpose of fitting her pliant softness to a more intimate nicety with his own increasingly urgent need, and allowing him to move her to the bed without any awkwardness. Her arms wound more tightly around his neck, instinctively abetting the desire that was rampaging through both of them. His mouth left hers with a sigh of deep satisfaction and her long graceful throat bent to the sensual play of his lips as he turned to take the few necessary steps.

Jackie opened eyes that were carelessly sightless, until they met other eyes. Shock jack-knifed her limp body into violent rejection. 'Edmund!' she squeaked; then, in mounting horror, 'Robert!'

Her hands beat reflexively on Sunny King's broad shouders. 'Let me go! The boys ... Edmund! Robert! You come out here this instant!'

Sunny King took another step towards the bed.

'Let me go!' she shrieked. 'The boys are under the bed.'

That stopped him but he did not release her.

She clenched her hands into fists and banged them down on his shoulders in frustration, all desire raging into panic-stricken anger. How could she have been so weak as to succumb to Sunny King's seductive manoeuvres! And the boys had been watching them! For how long? All the time that she had been swept along in that whirlpool of passion?

'Put me down!' she commanded in shrill desperation.

Sunny King ignored her.

Jackie wriggled frantically against his hold. 'Robert and Edmund, get yourselves out here at once!' she cried, almost reduced to appealing for their help in freeing her from this terrible man.

She caught only a glimpse of their crawling bodies before Sunny King lowered her enough to smother her mouth with another kiss. She tried to heave herself away but to no avail. He had her head clamped to his with one immovable hand. She clutched his mane of hair and pulled with furious might.

'Beast!' she hissed at him as he finally freed her lips.

'Didn't you like it, Mum?' Edmund's voice held a note of disappointed curiosity.

'Certainly not!' she snapped, pushing angrily against the seemingly impervious strength of Sunny King's embrace. She glared at him, furious with herself for having momentarily fallen victim to his sexual expertise. 'You are the most depraved, disgusting man I've ever met. Now let me go!'

'Only when you tell the truth. Admit you enjoyed every minute of it.'

Still he held her pinned to him in flaunting intimacy. In front of her own children! She felt utterly humiliated. His arrogant disregard for her feelings spurred a wild rage. She beat at him with flailing fists, but that didn't seem to make any impression on him. He ducked and weaved his head, an insidious smile on his face.

She lifted back one dangling foot and kicked his shin as hard as she could. He only blinked. And kept smiling at her. Jackie felt as though she had broken a toe. 'Let me go!' she shrilled at him. 'You ... you ... troglodyte!'

'What's that mean?' he asked in mystification.

'Look it up in a dictionary, you ignoramus.'

He laughed, a soft mocking laugh that sent a tormenting tingle down her spine. Then very gently he placed her on her feet and released her. 'Do you feel better now?'

Her cheeks burned with shame as he made a covert adjustment to his swimming trunks, and then she stepped away, trembling with outrage. 'I won't feel better until I'm out of this ... this palace of perversion.'

His laughter goaded her into violent reaction. She wheeled on Robert and Edmund, grabbed their arms and marched them out of the room.

'I don't think it will be long before you're back, Mrs Mulholland.'

The cynical amusement in Sunny King's musical voice spurred a fierce determination never to have anything to do with him again. Not for any reason. Jackie hauled the boys into a faster stride. They practically had to trot to keep up with her. She barely drew breath until they were out of the house.

Robert and Edmund exchanged eye-signals as their mother plunged them all down the driveway to the road. Silence was definitely indicated. The state of temper was uncertain and now was not the time for pleading mitigating circumstances for their escapade.

For the whole two hundred metres or so up the road to their adjoining property, they trailed cautiously in her wake. When they reached the gateway and the house was only another thirty metres away, Robert felt it was time to try some mollifying tactic.

'You sure are a good fighter, Mum,' he said admiringly.

'She's not as good as Sunny King,' Edmund blurted out, earning a venomous look from his brother.

'Do not refer to me as she,' Jackie grated. 'I am not the cat's mother.' She glared at both of them. 'And the name of Sunny King is not to be spoken in front of me again.'

'Yes, Mum,' Robert agreed with alacrity, very relieved by this amazing decision of his mother's. How could she lecture them if Sunny King was not to be mentioned?

'Why not?' Edmund asked.

The stupid dope, Robert thought in exasperation, shaking his head at his younger brother behind his mother's back. Although Edmund was only fifteen months younger than himself, sometimes he acted like a thick-headed little kid. It was perfectly obvious that Sunny King had somehow got the better of their mother and she was mad as hell about it. Even madder about that than she was about their sneaking off.

'That man can only be a bad influence. You are never to step foot on his property again,' came the vehement edict.

By this time they had reached the front steps of the house. 'Now!' their mother snapped. 'Get off to bed. Both of you. And God help you if you move out of your room again tonight.'

She let them go and Robert gave Edmund a quick shove into the hallway to save any further gaffes on his part. 'Goodnight, Mum,' they chorused with careful respect.

More like good morning, Jackie thought sourly as she bent to drag the spare mattress back inside. The pillow rolled off it as she gave an exasperated yank to get the bedding through the doorway. She bit down on an irritable curse and completed the task of pushing the mattress into the hall cupboard before going back to retrieve the pillow.

The house was still airless. Still hot. She thought of the air-conditioned coolness of Sunny King's residence and felt a sharp stab of envy. She picked up the pillow. Her body was still jangling from the sexual arousal that had been so abruptly terminated. She hugged the pillow to her in a need for soft comfort and wandered slowly around to the veranda which faced Sunny King's property.

The rock band was blaring again, the lights undimmed, the party still in full swing. A brief, titillating encounter, that was all it had been. Damn him! Damn him for using her like that! She felt terrible. Apart from the dreadful indignity of having been sprung by her children in the thrall of sexual excitement, she was now suffering the pangs of sexual frustration.

It had been years since she had felt anything like the feverish urgency he had made her feel. She had successfully managed to repress all that ever since Geoff had died, and even in the last few years before her widowhood. It had been nice, but not exactly frantic. Really, she hadn't experienced such quivering expectancy since ... since before Robert was born. In the latter years of her marriage ... Well, the plain truth was, Geoff had never been so provocatively sexy as Sunny King.

But she had loved Geoff. And she certainly didn't love that egomaniac, Sunny King. Furthermore, she wasn't going to have anything to do with him. She didn't need sex so much that she had to stoop to the likes of him for a tumble in bed. That was all it would be. He'd probably done it to a thousand women.

There were other, better men around than him if she wanted a lover. Men who would value her as a person and not just a convenient body. She hadn't really been looking for anyone since Geoff's death, but maybe she should. The boys wouldn't be with her for ever. If Sunny King found her attractive, then surely she could attract someone more compatible, someone who would be happy to share the rest of her life. Everything, not just bed!

She gritted her teeth in disgust at her unwarranted response to Sunny King and turned away to go back to her bedroom. Sleep was the immediate answer to the feeling that dreadful man had stirred. Tomorrow she would feel on top of herself again. One thing was certain: she was never going to let Sunny King get to her, not in any way whatsoever.

CHAPTER THREE

It was late Sunday afternoon before the exodus began from Sunny King's property. First the rock band in a gaily painted camper van; then, at intermittent intervals, two Jaguars, three Mercedes, four other camper vans, one Alfa Romeo, one Lamborghini, five rather insignificant station wagons, two Volvos and the rest of the list floated over Jackie's determined indifference, although Robert and Edmund persisted in keeping her informed. The highlight of the afternoon was the arrival and departure of a helicopter.

The party was over, which was the only welcome fact as far as Jackie was concerned. She felt like something the cat had dragged in and she desperately needed a good night's sleep. A cool change had come in from the south and apart from the occasional roar of a passing vehicle—did all Sunny King's friends have a passion for mad acceleration?—blessed silence had once again returned to the countryside.

On Monday morning she even awoke to the twittering of birds. She smiled, and it was the first smile to relax her taut facial muscles for over forty-eight hours. Everything was back to normal. Almost. She had been made too aware of unfulfilled needs to forget them in a hurry, but today she would get back to working on the clay in her pottery shed; a bit of pummelling would surely work off some of her inner frustration.

If only Sunny King had not bought the property next door! He was undoubtedly going to become a continual irritant, upsetting the contented tenor of her life. For all of ten years she had been happy here. Reasonably happy, she amended, not forgetting her horror and grief over Geoff's death. She certainly had no wish to go anywhere else or do anything other than what she was doing.

Which was something her parents had never understood, Jackie thought ruefully, remembering their disapproval at her lack of ambition. She did appreciate the broad and expensive education they had given her, and she had done very well at school, but somehow the continual living up to her parents' expectations had gradually palled, particularly since there had never been any time for other things.

Her parents had been so devoted to their own careers, Jackie had often wondered if she had been a mistake. Her mother had been thirty-seven at the time of Jackie's birth and really her parents had seemed to resent her intrusion into their lives. Certainly she had not felt important to them.

Not like with Geoff. He had shown her what love was all about. Geoff had cared about her feelings and had always made her feel valued as a person. She had never regretted her marriage to him. It did not matter that she had not gone on to art college, anyway. She had done quite well with her pottery without further tuition. And she always had time for her children. It was a good life that she had.

Except for missing Geoff.

But if Sunny King thought that her being a widow made her an easy prey, she would soon make him think again! That lecherous movie-mogul might have the golden touch but she could see his feet of clay. Clay . . . A smile of wicked satisfaction grew on Jackie's face as an inspired idea floated into her mind. Her pottery line of prehistoric animals was selling particularly well, but she was sick of doing dinosaurs. She would create something new, sort of like a llama with Sunny King's face on it. Definitely prehistoric.

The smile widened into a grin. She would fire it in the old brick-kiln behind the shed. Electricity wouldn't do for Sunny King. Definitely a wood fire, stoked to an absolute blaze of heat. It would be as good as burning an effigy.

Robert and Edmund were pleased to see their mother's easy-going humour restored. She was humming happily to herself as she worked on her clay and didn't even ask why they wanted the old sheets of galvanised iron from under the veranda. They were almost away scot-free when she commented absently, 'It's not another tree-house, is it?'

'No, Mum,' they assured her quickly, and raced off to begin building their canoe.

They all had a very satisfying few days without a ripple of disturbance on the home front. In fact, by Wednesday night Jackie had completely recovered her equanimity. Until the telephone rang and Sunny King's distinctive voice came over the line.

'I'm free tonight,' he said cheerfully.

Well, bully for you, Jackie thought sourly as she fought to retain her hard-won equanimity. 'Are they letting you out of your cage?' she drawled with sweet indulgence.

He chuckled. 'Don't you want to see me?'

She did her best to project airy indifference. 'No. Never again, thank you.'

'Ah, that's cruel to both of us. Why don't you face up to yourself and confess that we were made for each other? Come on over. Let's do something excitingly constructive. I can feel the surge of creativity in my veins. I know you're going to stir me to ...'

'No!' He was not going to stir her that way. She was not going to let him.

'Why not?' he asked reasonably.

'Because I couldn't stand what comes after it's finished.'

'What do you think is going to happen?'

'Once it was all over I'd be bored out of my mind. There is nothing more distressing than having had sex with someone who shares nothing else with you. You very quickly realise what a great mistake you've made. That's precisely what would happen with us.'

'How do you know that?' he asked, his voice accusing her of unwarranted fabrication.

'I read the divorce statistics.'

'I share a great deal with you. You give me a lot. There's not a chance that I'd be bored with you,' he argued.

She smiled, knowing that she had the drop on him for once. 'I know that. The problem is all on my side. I simply couldn't cope with you.'

There were several moments' silence before he admitted defeat. 'You are a first-class bitch, Mrs Mulholland,' he said cheerfully.

'No, I'm not, Mr King, but I can give a wonderful imitation of one when I put my mind to it.' And on that sweetly triumphant line she hung up on him.

However, Jackie's satisfaction frayed a little around the edges as she lay awake in her virtuous bed that night. She couldn't help wondering just how creative Sunny King might have been. Which disturbed her rather a lot, even though she was absolutely certain she had made the right decision. She pounded the clay considerably harder the next day.

A week went by, marked only by a fair increase in Jackie's potteryware and the great canoe disaster. The boys came trailing up from the river, their clothes dripping wet and their faces glum.

Jackie elicited the facts. They drove her to an exasperated outburst. 'How could you expect a canoe made out of galvanised iron to float?'

'Steel ships float,' Robert argued.

'It worked for a while,' Edmund added plaintively. 'We plugged up all the nail-holes with your modelling plasticine.'

This provocative revelation earned a daggers look from his elder brother.

Jackie sighed. Don't repress their spirit of adventure, Geoff had always said; boys will be boys. If they managed to grow up at all, they would most likely end up dying on the Matterhorn like their father, she thought dispiritedly, but nothing she said was going to change them. It was obviously in the blood.

And there were still another two weeks of the school holidays to get through. She prayed it would be without serious mishap. Perhaps they needed a spot of civilised culture to divert their minds from the more dangerous undertakings that seemed to attract them.

'We'll go to Parramatta tomorrow,' she decided brightly. 'You can go to the movies while I deliver my pottery and do some shopping.'

Robert's face lit with joy. 'Great, Mum! We've been dying to see *Live By The Sword*.'

'Yeah!' Edmund breathed ecstatically.

Jackie rolled her eyes in despair. She should have known better. It was bad enough that *Live By The Sword* was reported to be action-packed with gory violence, it was also the red-hot box office sequel to Sunny King's big hit, *Eye For An Eye*, which the boys had re-enacted in dangerous games ever since they had seen it three years ago. Another battery charge of Sunny King's one-eyed hero, Dirk Vescum, would probably result in two one-eyed children.

She tried. 'Wouldn't you like to see a comedy?'

They groaned. They argued. They invited her to go along with them and see for herself that there wasn't any harm in it. She couldn't win. Forbidding them to go would only earn their resentment, particularly since the movie had been rated for general exhibition. Every other kid from school would have seen it over the holidays. Jackie resigned herself to the inevitable, but a number of malevolent thoughts went winging their way to the property next door.

So much for civilised culture, she thought bitterly as she dropped the boys at the Village Cinema the next morning, but she cheered up considerably when the gift-shop agent raved over her Sunny King llamas. He wrote her out a lovely fat cheque, and, in a frivolous mood, Jackie bought herself a new sundress.

The boys' faces were still glowing with excitement when she picked them up and took them to Kentucky Fried Chicken for a late lunch. 'It was fantastic, Mum!' Edmund bubbled. 'You should have seen the part where Dirk Vescum cut their heads off.'

'I don't want to hear about it,' she said hurriedly.

'But it was only justice, Mum,' Robert pleaded. 'They deserved to be executed. They'd been torturing . . .'

'Robert! I said I don't want to hear about it!' Violence was totally repugnant to Jackie.

The boys bolted down their lunch and huddled together in the back seat of the car on the way home, whispering over the exploits of Dirk Vescum. Having excluded herself from the distasteful conversation, Jackie resented the fact that Sunny King had created anything that held her sons so enthralled. Him and his creativity! He couldn't lift his mind above the physical.

She was quite glad to reach Wiseman's Ferry and get out of the car while the punt took them across the river. The scenic beauty of the upper reaches of the Hawkesbury River always soothed her spirits: the lush river flats and the calm stretch of water, the thickly forested slopes rising behind them. Who would ever want to live in the city? she thought contentedly, as she breathed in the clean, fresh air.

The ferry ground to a halt and she climbed back into the car. She always enjoyed the drive to St Alban's even though the road was narrow and winding. One section of it was being resurfaced and there were signs up: PLEASE DRIVE SLOWLY, BEWARE OF WINDSCREEN DAMAGE. Jackie never drove at anything but a sedate pace, but she still automatically slowed down.

The car which zoomed past her was barely a blur, going at a faster speed than Toad of Toad Hall would ever have driven. Jackie heard it but she didn't get a chance to see it. With an almighty crack her windscreen shattered into thousands of crazed angles and she couldn't see anything at all. With her heart in her mouth she stamped her foot on the brake. The car came to a halt without hitting anything and she slumped over the wheel in relief.

'Wow! That was Sunny King's Lagonda. Can't he drive!' Edmund's voice was full of admiration.

'Anyone who had a car like that could drive as fast,' Robert observed scornfully.

Sunny King! He had done this to her! Jackie slammed out of the car, found a large stone and used it to punch a hole in the windscreen. The towering indignation she felt was compounded by her own children's feckless attitudes. Not even taking her side against that . . . that maniac! And all the money she had got from selling her work would go into replacing the windscreen. A hard, cold wrath rose inside her. Sunny King would pay for this, even if she had to hoist a stone through the windscreen of his precious Lagonda herself.

'I think Mum's mad,' Robert muttered to his younger brother as she flounced back into the car, her hand still curled around the stone she had been forced to use on her own car.

'Yeah,' Edmund breathed cautiously.

It was one of the world's greatest understatements. Driving with the broken windscreen was a nightmare; the rush of air against her face brought tears to her eyes. She fingered the rock she had placed beside her on the passenger seat. Sunny King was going to rue the way he had driven his car today.

By the time she reached his gateway, Jackie's anger was at an all-time high. Volcanic. The man represented everything she hated most. She stopped in front of his triple garage and alighted, the instrument of revenge in her hand. The garage doors were locked, unbudgeable, but Jackie was not to be defeated.

'You two boys stay in the car until I settle this business,' she ordered.

'This is really going to be something,' she heard Robert say gleefully.

But Jackie was already on her way, marching up to the front door of the house. She pressed her thumb on the door chimes and left it there. The door opened and Trevor Haines tried a welcome. 'Why, Mrs Mulholland ...'

'Get Mr Sunny King instantly.' Her tone of

voice dispensed with welcome.

'Uh, yes, Mrs Mulholland. Please wait here.' He swung away hastily.

Jackie didn't trust him. She wouldn't trust any of Sunny King's minions in a fit. She stepped forward into the foyer, snarling at the nude Greek statues as she did so. She saw Sunny King emerge from the second turret room, which was his study. He actually hummed a song as he jogged up the stairs towards her. His arms opened wide in welcome and an inane grin cut through his beard.

'Ah, Mrs Mulholland, how pleasant of you to drop in ...'

Her eyes beamed murder back at him. 'I've come for you.'

The grin widened. 'I knew you would. And I want to talk to you.'

'Take me to your garage.' The words were seethed through gritted teeth.

He blithely ignored them. 'The neglect you have shown over our common fence in recent years is deplorable.'

'I'll give you an *Eye For An Eye* ...'

He cocked his head on one side in mild consideration. 'Really, you're looking quite distressed. What's the matter?'

She weighed the stone in her hand with grim satisfaction. 'You're going to pay for what you did with your own brand of justice, Mr King. *Live By The Sword*, die by the ...'

'Are you threatening me?'

The lilting surprise in his voice fired the

explosion. 'Yes, I am! I'm going to give you back everything . . .'

He moved so quickly she had no time to strike at him or take any evasive action as he closed in on her. Her hand with the stone was pressed behind her back and her body imprisoned by a strong arm that held her against him like a vice. To her utter bewilderment he immediately started kissing her hair and forehead and uttering soft, soothing words.

'There, there, now. There's nothing that can't be sorted out. Given time. All we need is the right kind of communication. I know . . .'

'Don't do that to me!' she squawked in vehement frustration.

'I have to. It's the only way I can get you to talk sense.'

She was up against a bare chest. Bare thighs. He only had on a skimpy pair of shorts. Didn't he ever wear proper clothes?

'See? It's working, isn't it?' he crooned, his mouth working down to her nose. 'Let me kiss you properly.'

'I can't talk at all then,' she snapped furiously.

'Exactly.'

'I'll kill you,' she muttered, ducking her head low.

His mouth moved to her ear. 'Dear Mrs Mulholland, you've entranced me from the first moment I laid eyes on you. There's a certain charm, probably a backwardness in behaviour, that I find quite enchanting . . .' He nibbled at her ear-lobe.

'You ... you swine!'

'Combined with a marvellous vocabulary. Please let me help you. Pour your troubled soul out and I'll give it balm. Lift your head. Let me take away the pain. I'll kiss you as you should be kissed. With reverence. With passion. With ...'

He didn't mean a word of it. He was toying with her. Hatred for all he had done to her, what he was doing to her now, burnt up her throat and burst into spitting accusation. 'Your irresponsible driving could have killed us. Killed my children. You broke my windscreen and I'm going to break *your* damned windscreen if it's the last thing I do! That might teach you that the road doesn't belong entirely to you, you ...'

'I did that?' He let her go and stepped back a pace in astonishment.

'Yes, you did!'

His face was a picture of concern. He took her hand. 'Show me the damage.'

She wrenched her hand out of his and strode to his front door, pointing a quivering finger at her car. 'See? That's what you did!'

He obligingly followed and shook his head over the catastrophe. 'Oh dear!' His arm went comfortingly around her shoulders. 'You should always have laminated windscreens, my sweet. So dangerous not to have them.'

That was it! That was the last straw! Jackie's mind blew. Screeching like a banshee she swung her arm around, stone at the ready. Some last vestige of sanity prevented her from smashing it into his face. She wheeled and attacked the male nude statue, using her weapon like a sledge-hammer. The plaster cast crumbled under the attack.

'That's for starters,' she cried, swinging back to Sunny King, her eyes ablaze and her chest heaving from violent exertion. 'Now for the Lagonda!'

He stared at her, seemingly mesmerised by her fury for a brief instant. Then he was solemnly agreeing with her. 'You're quite right. So you should. I'll take you down to the garage. Come this way please.'

He led off down the curved staircase and, after a moment's startled pause, Jackie followed him. They went through the house, Sunny King gravely waving her on whenever she hesitated. He opened a door and stood back to usher her courteously into the triple garage.

Jackie sidled through the doorway, almost stumbling down the couple of steps to the garage floor in her anxiety to keep a reasonable distance between them, too suspicious of this placid accep-tance of Sunny King's to turn her back on him.

There's the Lagonda,' he nodded.

She backed a few paces away from him, then turned quickly. And there it was, right in front of her, the aerodynamic wedge shape so sleekly stylish, so beautifully proportioned, dazzling in its futuristic sophistication. She darted a wary glance back at the man behind her.

Sunny King sat on the step. 'Go ahead,' he invited.

Confusion weakened her rage. Why was he doing this? What game was he playing at? Somehow the initiative had slipped away from her, which wasn't fair. She worked hard on bolstering her fury. It was justified.

She strode around to the other side of the Lagonda, making sure that Sunny King couldn't play some last-minute trick on her. She balanced the stone in her grip, raised her arm. Doubts rocketed around her mind. She couldn't do it. It was wrong.

Her gaze wavered back to Sunny King. 'You really want me to do this to your car?' she asked hesitantly.

He made an open-handed gesture. 'If it makes you feel better.'

Jackie's brain whirled in dismay. How was she going to get out of this predicament with her pride intact? She looked at the fancy tinted winscreen of the Lagonda, fiercely reminding herself of the damage done to her own. Determination poised her arm to strike again, but she still couldn't do it. She glared at Sunny King, resenting his crazy passivity.

'No one else in the world would let me do this,' she shot at him in bitter accusation.

He shrugged. 'I'm not the same as anyone else.'

It was no use. She couldn't carry on with it. All the pent-up ferocity had drained out of her. She lowered her arm and, with a sigh of disgust at herself, dropped the stone on the floor. He had beaten her. Again! But a spark of fiery defiance rose from the ashes of defeat. She lifted her chin and met Sunny King's gaze with stubborn pride.

'I can't do it. It's wrong. Even so, I did you a favour over that statue. It was a crass piece of pseudo-art. And anyway, you started it, driving in a mad, reckless, irresponsible fashion. It's only because I cannot wittingly destroy something of real value that I'm not paying you back what you deserve.'

He nodded and stood up. 'I'll pay for your new windscreen. In fact . . .' He turned and shouted down the hallway. 'Trevor! Come down here please!'

The secretary came running.

'Trevor, I've inadvertently given Mrs Mulholland a great deal of distress. My fault. Please take her car, get a new windscreen installed, and pay for it.'

'Sure, Sunny.'

'And give her the keys to the Daimler. She'll need a car while her own is being repaired.'

'Right.'

'No, I . . . I can't,' Jackie protested, appalled by the generosity of what was being offered her, particularly in the wake of her own vengeful rage.

He swung his gaze to her. 'I insist.' Then he smiled as though happily struck with an idea that pleased him. 'Besides, I need your advice on a new statue.'

Shame crawled down her spine. She should never have lost her temper like that. There was no excuse for such wanton destruction. That act alone dismissed any debt that Sunny King owed her. She took a deep breath to counter the sick feeling growing inside her and shook her head at him. 'No . . . no, you can't . . . I won't . . .'

'Yes,' he said firmly. 'Trevor, the keys.'

The secretary rummaged in a drawer, found the

set he was looking for and brought them over to
Jackie, thrusting them into her hand. 'There you
are, Mrs Mulholland.'

'No. I . . .' He had turned away before she could
thrust them back. She felt stupidly helpless, robbed
of all resolve. Sunny King was doing it again,
taking all control out of her hands. Not letting her
have any say in the matter.

He started strolling towards her. 'Trevor, if
you'd go and fetch Robert and Edmund down here,
I'll look after Mrs Mulholland and show her how to
drive the car.'

The secretary obeyed him without question,
leaving Jackie alone in the garage with Sunny King
who opened the driver's door of the Daimler and
took up a casual stance by it.

'Please sit inside so I can familiarise you with the
controls,' he invited pleasantly.

Jackie tried once again to make an independent
stand. 'I really don't want . . .'

'If you don't get in, I'll pick you up and put you
in,' he continued just as pleasantly.

Mutiny stirred, stiffening her backbone. But one
look at the quirky little smile on Sunny King's face
reminded her that mutiny had not served her well
in dealing with him. It was either surrender her
pride or be subjected to further indignities, since he
had the advantage on her where physical strength
was concerned. She moved towards the car,
watching him warily. 'Promise not to touch me,'
she insisted.

'For the moment,' he agreed, devilment dancing
into the blue eyes.

She didn't trust him. Couldn't trust him. She quickly slid into the driver's seat and he shut the door on her, grinning openly as he rounded the bonnet to the passenger's side. Jackie stared at the polished walnut dashboard. How could she possibly accept the loan of a Daimler in place of her six-year-old Datsun? On the other hand, how could she get out of it when Sunny King had no scruples about pressuring her with physical blackmail?

He settled in beside her and slid an arm around her shoulders. Her pulse gave a panicky leap. Her eyes flew to his in mute protest but the laughing mischief that looked back at her was mesmerising in its sexy invitation.

'You promised not to touch me,' she half choked, her breath catching in her throat at his threatening nearness.

A hand came down on her thigh. 'The temptation was too great, and I want you to be happy.' The hand was caressing her thigh. His face was coming closer.

She didn't know whether to grab his hand away or push his head back. She just couldn't cope with Sunny King's aggressive tactics at all. 'Don't kiss me,' she cried, suddenly deciding the hand was the more disturbing factor.

'Of course not.' He lifted the offending hand out of her scrabbling grasp. 'I was just going to show you how to fix the seat belt. But now that you mention it ...'

The hand curved around her face, tilting it as his mouth came down to take possession of hers. He was doing it to her again, kissing her so damned persuasively that she didn't want to fight it. The feelings he was arousing were entirely sensual, sexual, all very physical. She couldn't possibly like the man. But he certainly was an expert at what he was doing.

She was co-operating in her own defeat, her mind told her plaintively. It told her to lift her free hand up to his shoulder and do something about it, since she was too weak to tear her mouth away from his. She lifted her hand, and his shoulder was smooth and round and nice to feel, and her hand slithered up, trying out a new course of its own.

His gentle hold on her face turned into a downward caress that found her breast, traced around it, did soft, pleasurable things to the tender fullness of it. She shouldn't allow it. She really shouldn't, Jackie's mind chided, but it did give her such a lovely melting feeling.

The noise of the children coming down the hallway jolted her out of the seductive spell he was weaving through her defences. Her eyes flew open in an urgent plea for discretion because she felt ridiculously helpless, her lips still throbbing with sensitivity, her body crying out for his touch. It was madness. He was a sex maniac on the loose. If he kept this up, there would come a time when she wanted his lovemaking, might even come to expect it.

He moved back, his hand dropping on to her thigh again, but only to give it a reassuring squeeze before it quickly withdrew. 'You're accustomed to driving automatic, aren't you?' he questioned in a casual voice, as if nothing at all had happened.

She looked dazedly at the gear lever. 'Yes,' she whispered, her voice as tattered as her defences.

The boys burst into the garage. 'Mum, are we really going to have the Daimler?'

'Yes,' Sunny King said emphatically.

Jackie felt hopelessly flustered, her eyes lifting to his in panicky appeal. 'Not really. If I hit any-thing ...'

He smiled. 'Consider your revenge complete.'

The man was impossible. She tried to think of other arguments, but Sunny King was telling the kids to pile into the back seat and Trevor Haines was passing over her handbag and handing the boys her shopping. She was not in control at all, and it didn't seem she ever would be around Sunny King. How could such an overbearing, abominable man reduce her to such ... such quivering jelly?

The boys hung over the front seats, excited and fascinated as Sunny King explained how the thermostat of the air-conditioning system worked, and the radio-cassette-player, and the hand brake and the alarm system. Jackie could hardly take it all in. She felt relieved when Sunny King got out to open the garage door, but felt too nervous to start the car. He came back to her window and smiled at her.

'Just turn the key in the ignition and put the gear into drive. No problem,' he assured her. 'And I'll see you tonight.'

'No.' She shook her head vehemently.

'Aw, come on, Mum,' Robert urged, not understanding.

Sunny King's smile tilted appealingly. 'About

the fences. Something's got to be done about them.
They're an eyesore.'

'No,' she repeated more sharply, desperate to
keep him at a distance until she had sorted herself
out. 'If you want something done about the fence,
do it yourself.' She started the engine to punctuate
the point.

He patted her shoulder. 'We'll discuss it tonight.
Bye now.'

The boys chorused back happy farewells and
Jackie drove out of the garage with a sinking feeling
of utter defeat. Somewhere along the line she had
lost the argument, lost her common sense, lost all
direction. How on earth was she going to handle
Sunny King tonight? She couldn't even handle
herself!

CHAPTER FOUR

'MUM, can we go abseiling with Trevor Haines?'
Robert asked eagerly, breaking into Jackie's agitated concentration over driving Sunny King's
Daimler.

It took her a couple of seconds to register the
question, then her mind instantly ballooned with
horror. 'No, you certainly cannot!'

'Why not?' Edmund demanded plaintively.

'You're not old enough,' Jackie snapped. 'I told
you that before.'

'Dad did it at our age,' Robert pointed out
reasonably.

'No! The answer is no!' Jackie repeated with a
vehemence that didn't allow any leeway for
argument.

Her emotions were all achurn as it was, and here
her children were, reminding her of Geoff's death.
The memory of that loss bit deep. Geoff, the
adventurer, the man to whom nothing was impossible, who wanted to experience everything that
would make any normal person flinch in fear. And
their children hero-worshipped his image, his
memory. It was terribly worrying, more worrying
than anything Sunny King could do to her.

On the other hand, both boys idolised Dirk
Vescum, the fantasy hero of Sunny King's movies.

And this handsome gesture of lending them a
Daimler ... it was sure to make the boys think
Sunny King was marvellous too. She shouldn't
have taken it. She shouldn't have responded to his
kiss. She shouldn't have done a lot of things. It was
very unsettling to find herself so vulnerable to a
man like Sunny King.

She drove the Daimler into the old shed that
served as a garage and felt slightly calmer as she
successfully brought it to a halt without mishap. It
was just plain stupid her having this car at all. She
didn't need it; her own would surely be repaired by
tomorrow afternoon. She would make Sunny King
take it back tonight—it was too big a favour for her
to accept. Perhaps he was expecting it to buy her
favour. Wasn't that the type of tactic movie moguls
used to woo their women?

Jackie was out of the luxury car as fast as a
scalded cat. She hurried into the sanctuary of her
own home, telling herself she would never, never,
never stoop to becoming one of Sunny King's
women. Even if he was a handsome devil with sex
appeal galore, she had had plenty of evidence about
his character and that was all bad. There was no
doubt that there had to be a devious motive behind
his generosity. Any involvement with Sunny King
could only bring her grief.

Jackie sighed in irritation as she noticed that the
house was in a mess. Too many hours spent in the
pottery shed, she berated herself, although she had
to acknowledge that she wasn't the greatest
housekeeper in the world at the best of times. The

boys only compounded the problem, leaving things lying around if she didn't hound them. In a tone of voice that brooked no excuses, she ordered a general clean-up.

She wasn't doing this for Sunny King, Jackie told herself. It didn't matter what he thought of her home. It didn't matter what he thought of her either. It was simply a matter of pride and self-respect that she made the living-room as tidy as possible. Then, having finished with the evening meal, she felt constrained to give the kitchen a thorough cleaning.

However, all the scrubbing in the world couldn't scrub out her concern over having to face Sunny King again. He always seemed to turn the tables on her in the most disconcerting manner. Her concern grew into resentment. It was an intrusion, his coming over here. She hadn't invited him; she didn't want him to come. In fact, there was no reason why she had to put up with it, and she wouldn't.

With an air of righteous decision she telephoned Sunny King's residence. Trevor Haines answered the call and she took the opportunity of asking about her car.

'Everything's fine, Mrs Mulholland. No problem. It'll be fitted with a laminated windscreen.'

She frowned over the generosity of the replacement but there was nothing she could do about it now. 'When will I have it back, Mr Haines?'

'Oh, please call me Trevor, Mrs Mulholland. The boys do. And I'm afraid it won't be back for a week or so. Some hold-up with the manufacturers. But not to worry. Sunny doesn't need the Daimler for anything.'

A week! And she would have to do food shopping before the weekend. She needed the use of a car, damn it! 'May I please speak to Mr King?'

'Well, er, he's not available at the moment, Mrs Mulholland. May I take a message?'

Jackie sighed in irritation. What was he doing that he wasn't available? Seducing the cook? She had to stop him from coming over here. Just the thought of seduction was enough to unnerve her. She spoke as firmly as she could.

'Mr King said he was coming over here tonight to discuss our common fence. Please tell him I have no intention of paying for a new fence and if he desperately wants one, he'll have to pay for it himself. The matter is not open for discussion so he can save himself a visit.'

'Could you hold the line a minute, Mrs Mulholland?'

He was gone before she could close the conversation and Jackie's irritation rose as she waited.

'Er, Mrs Mulholland?'

'Yes,' she snapped.

'Sunny said to tell you that he's recognised his Waterloo, even if you haven't, and he has no inclination to save himself. He said he'll talk to you about it when he sees you.'

Her mind buzzed with angry retorts but Trevor Haines was merely the messenger boy and it was obvious that Sunny King was not going to be put off. 'Thank you,' she said politely and slammed the telephone down.

She sat there taking deep breaths to counter the skitterish feeling that was fluttering through her veins. He was coming—she couldn't stop him—and he wouldn't listen to her. She knew he wouldn't. He would just . . . She jumped to her feet and strode into the living-room where the boys were sprawled on the floor watching television.

'Robert! Edmund!'

They turned up expectant faces.

'These are your orders. You are not, I repeat not, under any circumstances whatsoever, to leave me alone with Sunny King. Do you understand?'

'Yes, Mum,' they chorused. They exchanged mystified looks as their mother strode off to her bedroom, then dismissed the matter with expressive shrugs and turned their attention back to *Mysteries Of The Deep*.

Jackie felt hot and bothered and grubby from cleaning the kitchen. She took a quick shower and put on the new sundress she had bought, not because she wanted to look attractive for Sunny King, but because it made her feel better. It was a nice dress with a fresh lime-green and white floral print, and she was entitled to wear a nice dress if she wanted to.

However, the shoestring straps did leave her shoulders bare and the neckline was a trifle low, revealing just the slightest swell of her full breasts. But she was certainly not going to be ruled by what Sunny King might think.

Waterloo indeed! She didn't believe for a minute that she had conquered his heart. Sunny King lived in a fantasy world—his dreadful house was witness to that—and if she was ever fool enough to believe his extravagant talk, that would be her Waterloo. If she succumbed, how long would their relationship last? Two hours at most. And then how would she feel?

Jackie found herself remembering how she had felt this afternoon in the Daimler. Two hours of Sunny King's lovemaking... She hurriedly clamped down on the tempting thought. It was madness. What she had to remember was all his deficiencies in character, and she had ample proofs of those. She couldn't possibly surrender her self-respect to such a man.

On that note of proud determination she swept out to the kitchen, made herself a cup of coffee and joined the boys in the living-room. She tried to concentrate on the television programme but her gaze kept drifting to the clock and her ears were listening for the sound of the Lagonda.

The programme ended at eight-thirty. The boys then chose to watch an old western movie. Time crept on ... nine o'clock ... nine-fifteen ... nine-thirty ... Jackie's nerves were frayed to snapping point. It was just what she should have expected from Sunny King, an ill-mannered, uncivilised notoriety seeker. No consideration. He would keep the whole world waiting without a thought for anyone but himself.

Maybe he had decided to take her at her word

and wasn't calling at all. The thought brought an odd feeling of anti-climax. Almost disappointment. No, it was relief, Jackie told herself decisively. Then the vibrant resonance of a well-tuned engine assailed her ears and her heart leapt into her throat.

The squeal of tyres and the sound of sprayed gravel ricocheting around the garden left no doubt on the matter. Sunny King had arrived. Jackie bit her lips. The man was an ass, an extroverted show-off with the mentality of a child. She stood up, gathered her dignity about her, walked down the hallway, switched on the outside light and opened the front door.

He got out of the car and Jackie was relieved to see that he was fully clothed for once, however eccentric his fashion choice was: loose white trousers that suggested pyjama bottoms and a baggy white shirt with pockets everywhere and only one button done up near his waist. A couple of fine gold chains gleamed on the expanse of tanned chest on show.

He grinned at her, eyes sparkling with devilish anticipation. 'Sorry to be early. I didn't want to disturb the children before you sent them to bed, but in the end I couldn't wait any longer.'

Early! Jackie immediately bristled at the implications of his blithe greeting. It certainly wasn't early for an innocent discussion of fences and she could only think of one reason why he wanted the boys out of the way. He was closing the gap between them rapidly, bounding up the steps to the veranda. Jackie retreated a pace into the hallway.

'The boys don't go to bed early during school holidays. They're waiting up for you.' It gave her enormous satisfaction to slap that information in his face and even more satisfaction to see that it halted him in his tracks.

But only for a moment. He stepped forward, lifted his arms and hung his hands on the lintel above the door, seeming to flaunt his body at her with arrogant confidence in his own attractions. And God help her, she did find him strongly attractive, and he knew it! But it was only physical, Jackie fiercely reminded herself.

'In that case, I think we should go down and inspect the fences. Together. Alone. So you can see at first hand what I mean.' The soft words sang with suggestiveness.

Her pulse pounded into overdrive. There could be no doubt about his intentions now. A roll in the grass would do him if he couldn't have an immediate tumble in bed. 'I'll call the boys,' she said quickly and was already turning when a hand dropped on to her shoulder, making her pause, causing her heart to play leapfrog with itself.

'Don't do that,' he said quietly. The hand slid away, with a finger lightly tracing a shoestring strap to the soft swell of breast. 'I like your dress. It suits you,' he added with a winning smile.

She was not going to be putty in his too-experienced hands. Jackie retreated another pace, out of easy reach. She took a deep, steadying breath and gave it to him straight. 'Mr King, you seem to have the wrong idea about me. I might be a widow but I'm not available to jump into bed with the first man who comes along; and certainly, if I had any inclination along those lines, that man wouldn't be you.'

He laughed at her.

She desperately hung on to her dignity. 'Now, please do be sensible, Mr King.'

His eyes sparkled. 'Be a devil. Let yourself go.'

'Can't you think of anything else?' she demanded in exasperation.

'Not when I'm with you,' he grinned.

'Don't be ridiculous!' she snapped, losing patience with him and doing her best to shut off the wicked thoughts that were popping into her mind.

'From the first moment I saw you ...'

'The answer is no!'

'... I promised myself that you would be my woman.'

'No, no, no!'

His eyebrows slanted appealingly. 'You must realise that at heart I'm the last of the great romantics. That's why I'm so successful. And that's why you appeal to me so much.'

'I've never heard such bombastic nonsense in all my life,' Jackie scorned.

He dropped his other hand from the lintel and Jackie retreated another pace. Words weren't a problem. She was in control as long as they were just trading words, but if he got too close she might be in trouble, no matter what her mind said. He leaned against the door-jamb and slowly, deliberately folded his arms, all the time grinning at her, mocking her fear.

'I think I'll make a movie about our relationship,' he said whimsically.

'We haven't got a relationship,' she answered loftily.

He chuckled and reached out an inviting hand. 'It would be a huge success. Now come down and look at the fences with me. I have a vision ...'

'You are preposterous!'

'I'm going to knock it all down. Everything.'

She shook her head in confusion. 'Knock what down?'

He made a sweeping gesture. 'The fence is the first to go. Then that ugly brick kiln and the ramshackle sheds ...'

'No,' Jackie breathed in disbelief.

'Then this house. Knock 'em all down. Bring in the biggest bulldozer you've ever seen. Raze 'em to the ground.'

Her hands planted themselves on her hips in indignation. 'Don't even dare to think such a thing! This is my home and ...'

'Think what a superb view I'll have when they're all gone.' He refolded his arms and his whole body emanated smugness.

Jackie stamped her foot at him. 'You're crazy! This is crazy talk!'

He blithely ignored the accusation.

She flounced to the opposite side of the hallway, leaned her back on the wall, folded her own arms and glared at him. 'I'd never permit it and you wouldn't get away with it.'

His eyes laughed at her. 'That's what I was told before I made *Eye For An Eye*. Impossible. Can't be done. But I did it. Our children ...'

'You haven't got any children.'

'That's why we have to get started as soon as possible. How old are you, anyway? Must have been a child-bride. Plenty of years for us to ...'

'Will you stop this?' Jackie shrilled, sheer incredulity driving her voice high. 'You don't even know me. And I don't like you. How can you talk about us having children?'

He gave her a look of reproach. 'Take the grand approach to life. Don't think in trivia. You know you want me. We'd make a great couple.'

Jackie took a deep, calming breath. For some unaccountable reason her heart was leaping all over the place. 'Are you actually proposing to me?'

His smile was pure lechery. 'When we touch our minds are in harmony. You have the loveliest breasts I've ever seen. And the grandest hips. What more can a man want? I'll make you mine and never let you go.'

Nothing but sex on his mind! Just as she had thought. A lot of empty words just to get her to go to bed with him. She had to end his little game before he got her confused again.

'Mr King, your imagination has run riot. The answer to all your propositions is no, no, no, and no! You're not knocking my fence down. If you come near my kiln, or my sheds, or my house, with your bulldozer, I'll blast you with both barrels of my shotgun. And anyone who cohabited with you would have to be certifiably insane.'

He looked peeved. 'You don't like me much yet, do you?'

'That is a masterpiece of meiosis.'

'What's that mean?' he demanded suspiciously.

'Understatement,' Jackie replied with succinct satisfaction. 'I find you abhorrent, rude ...'

'Now hold on there! You're a mite rash with your words. I looked troglodyte up in the dictionary, and I'm not at all like a primitive gorilla.'

But Jackie's tongue was in full spate, recklessly intent on hitting back at him for threatening her. 'We don't all see ourselves as others see us,' she quipped.

'You'll come to see my good points.'

'I doubt it.'

He unfolded his arms and straightened up and his eyes held a purposeful gleam. 'I can see we need some other form of communication. Kiss me.' He took a step towards her.

'Robert! Edmund! Come here this instant,' she shrieked.

'We're just here, Mum,' Robert answered promptly, and she turned to see both boys levering themselves up from the floor on either side of the doorway into the living-room. It was only then that she realised that the television was off.

'Have you been listening?' she demanded, absolutely appalled at the thought.

Robert took it upon himself to reply. 'You told us we weren't to leave you alone with Sunny King, Mum, so when you didn't bring him in, and you didn't call us out, we thought we'd better hold a watching brief.'

Oh, God! Hoist on her own petard! They'd heard every word!

Sunny King chuckled. 'Well, well, well! How very interesting to find out that you can't trust yourself alone with me, Mrs Mulholland.'

I'll kill them, Jackie thought wildly. If they don't kill themselves I'll surely do those boys in. She swung back to Sunny King, breathing fire. 'It's you I don't trust. And let me tell you that anyone who trespasses on my property is going to get blasted.'

He sobered, but fixed her with a determined eye. 'The fence goes.'

'Only if you're prepared to replace it at your own expense.'

'Then the kiln.'

'Just you try it and see what you get!'

'Then the house.'

'Over my dead body!'

'And then you. I'm going to take you under my wing and give you all you deserve.'

'Please go before I lose my temper, Mr King.'

'I wish you sweet dreams of love. I'll win, you know.'

'Not bloody likely!'

He laughed and gave her a mocking wave of farewell. 'Goodnight, my love.'

'Goodbye!' she yelled after him, but only his laughter answered her.

She slammed the front door shut, snapped off

the outside light and wheeled on her two sons. Their eyes were alive with fascinated interest and she felt pinned by them, unable to explain or excuse the conversation they had overheard.

Edmund broke the impasse, speaking with a respect he rarely showed. 'Mum, that was the greatest adult conversation we've ever listened to. Much better than the TV.'

Robert offered a more critical viewpoint. 'Why didn't you say yes, Mum? We think it would be terrific to have Sunny King as our father.'

'Bed!' she croaked and swallowed hard to get more authority in to her voice. 'Go to bed. I don't want to discuss what you've heard. I don't want you to talk about it. Just forget Sunny King and go to bed. Right this minute.'

'But ...' Edmund began, and received a swift kick to the ankle from Robert.

'OK, Mum. Night,' he said tactfully.

'Night, Mum,' Edmund echoed obediently.

'But she kissed him the other night,' Jackie heard him hiss at Robert as they went off to their bedroom.

She sagged back against the front door and ran a trembling hand over her forehead. She had to pull herself together. She never lost her temper. Hardly ever. She was an easy-going person, almost placid. She had calmly dealt with everything life had tossed up to her—until now.

It hadn't been easy. Being married to Geoff had had its problems. He had never been very organised over domestic affairs, and she had kept everything in order when he was off on his expeditions. She was really a very level-headed, capable woman, not given to panic or any excesses in temperament.

So how come Sunny King could make her fall to pieces?

It was ridiculous; it had to stop. She couldn't carry on like this. Not only was he undermining her own sense of security but he was undermining her relationship with her children, making her feel a fool in front of them. He was not to be let near her again, even if she had to stop him with the ultimate weapon. Him and his bulldozer. Just let him try! She'd get him with both barrels of the shotgun all right.

CHAPTER FIVE

Two days later the bulldozer turned up. Jackie immediately went to the gun cupboard, unlocked it, found the cartridges for the shotgun and loaded it. She stalked out to the veranda, all primed to protect hearth and home. If Sunny King's henchmen came anywhere near the kiln or the sheds or the house with their bulldozer, they'd be met with more than verbal resistance. By God they would!

The bulldozer headed straight for the fence. The old posts went down like matchsticks before the might of the machine, and within an hour the fence was gone. The bulldozer dug a large hole and buried the lot. Jackie didn't mind the dangerous strands of rusty barbed wire being safely disposed of under a metre of earth, but the posts could have been used for firewood. The utter wastefulness of it fed her resentment of Sunny King's high-handed actions.

The bulldozer started trundling up the old fence-line. Jackie raced down to the brick kiln and took up guard, but the monstrous machine did not deviate from its route. The driver gave her a cheery wave as he went past. She followed him up to the road and saw the bulldozer reloaded on its float-truck.

'You're not coming back?' she demanded suspiciously.

'Do you want a job done?' the operator asked. 'Save you the cost of floating the 'dozer if I do it now.'

'No, thank you. I just want to know if you're finished here, or if Mr King has other orders for you.'

'Not today he hasn't. Just get rid of the fence.' He gazed down the bare line with satisfaction. 'All neat and tidy for him. Starting on the new one this afternoon, he said.' He nodded at the gun. 'Shooting rabbits?'

'No. Just ready for trespassing llamas,' she retorted grimly.

The operator gave her a wary look that wondered if she'd lost her marbles, said a hasty goodbye, and swung up into the cabin of his truck.

Jackie didn't care what he thought. She was glad to see him and his bulldozer leave and know that they weren't coming back. Not today, anyway. She locked up the shotgun and headed down to the pottery shed, needing some activity to relax her taut nerves.

Usually she found working with clay very soothing but she couldn't get her mind concentrated on it at all. Thoughts of Sunny King kept distracting her, making her more and more irritable, and her work suffered accordingly. When she went up to the house to have some lunch, the boys were already in the kitchen cutting sandwiches, their clothes absolutely filthy and their hands only given a token washing.

'If I've told you once, I've told you a thousand times, do not touch food with dirty hands,' she ordered, doing her best to hold on to her frayed temper. 'What in the world have you been doing to get yourselves in such a mess?'

'Playing in the dirt the bulldozer dug up. It's great for making roads and things,' Robert explained with unabashed enthusiasm.

'We're making a Grand Prix race-track,' Edmund chimed in. 'And we did wash our hands, Mum.'

They grabbed their sandwiches and zoomed out of the door before she could voice any protests or point out any more deficiencies in hygiene. With a sigh of exasperation, Jackie wiped up the dusty footprints on the kitchen floor and harboured thoughts of sending the dirty laundry over to Sunny King. Except he would have someone else do it.

Then the truckload of new fence-posts arrived, along with a pole-driving machine that fired them into the ground with the force and noise of a cannon. Jackie brooded through the barrage of sound, having abandoned all hope of doing any creative work. Another truck arrived and a team of fencing contractors got to work, bolting railings to the posts.

No ordinary wire fence for Sunny King, Jackie thought sourly, but, as she watched it go up, she had to admit it was a vast improvement on the old one. Undoubtedly he would have it painted white like the rest of the fences on his property. The cost of maintenance wouldn't worry him. All he cared about was his view.

She walked outside and took a long, hard look at what Sunny King saw of her place. It was an old house and the paint was peeling. It had seemed so charming when she and Geoff had bought it ten years ago. Boys should be brought up in the country, he had said, and of course she had agreed with him. Still agreed. But old places needed looking after and she didn't have the money to do it.

When Geoff had died he had left her the unencumbered property and a small insurance policy which her investment adviser had managed to good effect, but the income was only enough for subsistence living. Her pottery paid for the running of the car and the extra things the boys required from time to time, but it was going to take a lot of pottery to get the house re-painted.

And the sheds did look ramshackle. The garage walls had a slight lean and the doors didn't meet properly. The roofing was rusty and leaked in places. As for the kiln, she supposed it did look ugly, with its blackened bricks. Nevertheless, it still worked, and that was the main thing.

The thought didn't do much to lift Jackie's spirits. Depression rolled over her as she considered the future. Robert was starting high school this year and Edmund wasn't far behind. Life was not going to be so simple for ever. She had to do something about getting them on to a better financial footing.

Whether they sensed her inner distress or not Jackie did not know, but the boys were particularly helpful and considerate that night, doing the washing up after tea and going to bed early without being told. It did surprise her when they begged off going shopping in the Daimler the next morning, but she was inwardly relieved that she didn't have to worry about their fooling around in Sunny King's car. She assumed that the Grand Prix race-track was still under construction.

Jackie was too nervous about driving the Daimler to go all the way to the supermarket in Windsor. She could buy most of what she needed at Wiseman's Ferry and she would make do until her own car was returned, even if the food did cost a bit more. It was a mistake she very soon regretted. Having lived in the area for over ten years, all the local people knew her and her possession of a Daimler raised eyebrows.

'Got a new car, Mrs Mulholland,' the ferry master observed. 'Very nice. Very nice indeed,' he added, his eyes full of dollar question marks.

'No, it's not mine,' she said hurriedly. 'I've just got the loan of it while mine's being repaired.'

'Very obliging garage!' he commented drily.

'Not the garage. My, er, neighbour lent it to me.'

'Very obliging neighbour.' His eyes sharpened with speculation. 'Sunny King bought next to you, didn't he?'

'Yes, that's right,' she muttered, a tide of

warmth creeping up her neck.

'A-hah. Become good friends, have you?'

'Just neighbours,' Jackie grated.

And that was only the beginning. It was the same everywhere she went. Sunny King's generosity fired everyone's imagination. It didn't matter how she tried to explain it, she could see that her reputation was ruined; no one was going to believe that there wasn't something going on between her and Sunny King. She was on the verge of tears all the way home.

The boys didn't answer her call so she had to carry the parcels in by herself, which added to her feeling that the whole world was against her. They were late coming up from the paddock for lunch, too, and when she walked down to the back yard to yell out to them, they were nowhere to be seen. Gone for a dip in the river, Jackie decided, and didn't worry about them. They could both swim like fish and no doubt they would appear when they were hungry enough.

But they didn't appear, and by three o'clock Jackie felt annoyed enough to walk down to the river. There was no sign of them and no answer to her calls. Anger built with every step back to the house. They were supposed to leave a note if they were going to a friend's house. Hadn't she drummed that into them? She'd teach them a lesson all right. They could come on home right now, no matter what marvellous game they were playing.

However, several telephone calls elicited the fact

that none of their friends had seen either Robert or
Edmund all day. Jackie's anger gathered an edge of
anxiety. Where the devil were they and what were
they doing? Could they have got themselves into
trouble? They were not stupid, she told herself;
adventurous but not stupid. If one was hurt the
other would go for help. No need to panic.

But her anxiety mounted as hour after hour
crawled by. She took to pacing the veranda on the
lookout for them. Teatime came and went. Anxiety
built into fear. What would she do if they hadn't
come home by dark? Where could they be?

The sun was setting when she finally spotted
them, running across the paddock beyond the new
fence. The sick relief she felt churned into
monumental anger. They were on Sunny King's
property, coming from the direction of Sunny
King's house. That irresponsible, feckless playboy
was at the bottom of this escapade.

Robert waited at the fence for Edmund who was
lagging badly, obviously exhausted from whatever
they had been doing. They had angled their run so
that their approach would be from the direction of
the river and Jackie went to greet them at the back
door. Robert was talking fast and furiously to
Edmund, who was nodding wearily. They did not
see their mother until she spoke.

'And just where have you been?' she demanded
in an ominous tone.

'Sorry, Mum. We didn't realise how late it was
getting,' Robert babbled at high speed.

'You haven't answered my question, Robert.'

'We went bird-watching.'

Which was an out and out lie! She could see evasion written all over their faces.

'Oh, and what birds did you see, Edmund?' she asked silkily.

'Er ... kookaburras, magpies, cockatoos, rosellas and ... er ... lots more.'

'Well, that's very interesting. I didn't think Sunny King would be interested in birds of the feathered kind.'

'He didn't go with us, Mum,' Edmund denied stoutly.

'Then who did go with you, Edmund?'

He suddenly realised he had fallen into a trap and looked at Robert for guidance.

Robert reluctantly shouldered the responsibility. 'It was Trevor Haines, Mum.'

Trevor Haines ... Jackie's mind whirred and clicked. She turned and fired straight at Edmund. 'Did you go abseiling?'

The shock on his face gave the game away. Jackie was so furious, she couldn't trust herself to speak. She pointed inside and the boys quickly ducked under her arm and raced for the bathroom. Jackie went into the kitchen to prepare tea for them. There was murder in her heart.

How dared Sunny King and Trevor Haines involve her children in something as spectacularly dangerous as going up and down cliffs on ropes? They should be strung up on ropes themselves. Of course the boys had to be punished for their disobedience, but the main blame could be laid

fairly and squarely on the doorstep of 'King's
Folly'. And the leader in that folly was surely
Sunny King.

So this was his next move, seducing her sons
away from her authority! Getting them on his side
so she couldn't look to them for any support against
him. How underhand could he get, just to win his
own way?

When the boys finally presented themselves, all
scrubbed up and in their pyjamas, they looked so
tired, Jackie didn't have the heart to take them to
task tonight. Besides, she was immensely relieved
to have them home safe and sound. Lectures and
punishment could wait until tomorrow. And she
would have a few choice words to say to Trevor
Haines and Sunny King tomorrow, too.

The boys slept late the next morning and Jackie
had only just finished laying down the law to them
when the now-familiar sound effects of Sunny
King's driving heralded his arrival in the front
yard. The blast of the Lagonda's horn to reinforce
the announcement did nothing to lighten Jackie's
mood. She went straight to the gun cupboard and
armed herself with the shotgun. Sunny King was
just alighting from his car when she stepped out on
the the veranda.

'Good morning!' he called cheerfully as he
caught sight of her. 'Lovely morning, isn't it?'

Jackie moved to the top of the front steps and
pointed the gun at him. 'Stay right where you are,
Mr Sunny King. Don't move another step!'

He looked startled for a moment then mockingly

raised his hands. 'What kind of reception is this? Just when we've got on to first name terms too. I've been wanting to hear my name on your lips ever ...'

'Just what did you think you were doing with my children yesterday?' she cut in savagely.

'I did nothing. Trevor took them abseiling. He told me they really enjoyed themselves. Now please put the gun down and let me come on to the veranda. It's hot out here in the sun.'

'You can bake in hell for all I care. You knew about this abseiling, didn't you? You let them go. You didn't care if they fell and broke their necks,' she accused with venom.

'What's all the fuss about? They got home safely, didn't they?'

'No thanks to you. You don't care about anyone but yourself.'

'Now that's not true ...'

But Jackie wasn't listening. She was in full spate. 'I haven't known a moment's peace since you started building that damned whorehouse over there. Now you just get back in your car and get out of my life. And you can send your equally irresponsible secretary over here to pick up your other damned car, too. I don't want it.'

His hands lowered into a gesture of appeal. 'Please put the gun down and let's talk about ...'

'I don't want to talk to you.'

'I have a proposition ...'

'The answer's no.'

'You haven't heard it yet.'

'It doesn't matter.'

His hands dropped to his hips and he shook his head at her in reproof. 'I won't take no for an answer. You've tried and convicted me in a kangaroo court and now I'm going to open your mind.'

He stepped forward. Jackie swung the gun up to her shoulder and cocked it. 'Take one more step and I'll shoot.'

He stopped and heaved a sigh. 'OK, I don't mind dying in the cause of love. Where are you going to shoot me?'

'In the stomach.'

He considered her with a critical eye. 'That would be more than painful.'

'Dead right!'

'Can't we reach a compromise?'

'No.'

He huffed in exasperation, seemed about to swing away, then had the gall to grin at her. 'I'm coming to get you.'

Her heart did something curious and there was a rush of blood to her head. 'Don't try it,' she screeched.

He stepped forward. The blast of the gun spun Jackie around. The noise stunned her into immobility.

'God almighty! You fired it!'

The shocked utterances from Sunny King sped Jackie's recovery. 'That was a warning shot,' she declared shakily. 'Be grateful I didn't hit you.'

'Grateful!' he roared at her. 'I felt the bloody

pellets whizzing past my head, you crazy woman!'

He started towards her, vengeful purpose written all over him.

'I'll shoot again,' she screamed. 'I've still got one barrel left.'

Edmund came pelting out on to the veranda, yelling at the top of his voice. 'Robert! Come and look at this! Mum's trying to kill Sunny King.'

That did it. The split second of lapse in concentration as she looked at Edmund allowed Sunny King to get to her. The shotgun was torn from her hands and hurled away. Then he was lifting her up, shaking her, his face working with fury as he spouted forth a stream of righteous anger.

'Call me irresponsible! How mad can you get, shooting to maim and kill? I'm going to wallop your bottom until it puts some sense in your head. I'm going to wallop it until your brain thinks straight. I'm going to give you something you'll remember me by for the rest of your life. And thank me for it. I'm going to . . .'

'No, no, no!' Jackie wailed, arms flailing, legs kicking—but to no effect.

He was hoisting her into a position to carry out his threat, words still frothing from his mouth. Jackie tried to catch at the veranda post in a vain attempt to keep herself upright. She looked desperately around for some other form of help as he started to lower himself into a sitting position on the front step. What she saw froze the blood in her veins.

'Edmund! she screamed. 'Put that gun down!'

Sunny King sat down with thump, Jackie strewn across his lap. The flow of words had ceased with her frightened shriek. He stared at Edmund who had picked up the shotgun and was pointing it at them.

'God Almighty!' Sunny King breathed in horror. 'The whole family's mad.' He raised his voice to a bull-like roar. 'Point the bloody thing at me, you stupid boy, not at your mother.' Then suddenly he was rolling, taking Jackie with him, shielding her with his body. 'Bring that gun to me,' he commanded.

'You're going to hurt my mother,' Edmund retorted in stubborn defiance.

'I'm not hurting your mother. I'm protecting her from her idiot son. Bring that gun over here and give it to me.'

Half-smothered as she was, Jackie struggled for breath. 'Do as he says, Edmund,' she gasped. 'If I'd wanted him shot I'd have done it myself.'

Edmund remained steadfast. 'Dirk Vescum wouldn't give up,' he declared.

Sunny King muttered a vicious curse. 'Dirk Vescum hates violence!' he roared. 'He certainly wouldn't do anything that could endanger innocent people's lives. Now hand over that goddamned gun, and I'll get off your mother. You're the one who's hurting her.'

'Better do as he says, Edmund,' Robert put in.

The aim of the gun wavered away as Edmund glanced up at his brother. 'He's pretty big and he's really angry,' Edmund argued.

'There's three of us against him,' Robert pointed out. 'Give it over.'

The barrel dragged on to the ground as Edmund reluctantly did Robert's bidding. Sunny King snatched it from him, sprang to his feet, strode out to the front yard and fired it into the air, emptying it of ammunition.

The anguish that Sunny King had caused her over over the last few days suddenly combined with the fear of the last few minutes, and Jackie gave vent to it all as she climbed to her feet. 'See what you do with your rotten Dirk Vescum movies!' she shrieked.

'What I do!' he bellowed in fierce indignation. 'My God! Just wait till I get my hands on you.'

Jackie shrank back as he wheeled on her in a towering rage. Robert leapt the veranda railing and put himself between them. He was instantly joined by Edmund, both of them with their fists raised ready to fight. It brought Sunny King up short.

'We're not going to let you hurt our mother,' Robert stated belligerently.

Sunny King shook his head in disbelief. 'They're all mad. Not a grain of sense anywhere.' He raised his gaze to Jackie, blue eyes blazing. 'And I came over here to do you a favour!' he roared.

'I don't want your two-faced favours,' she screamed back at him. 'The best favour you can do for me is to go away and stay away.'

His mouth clamped into a grim line as he briefly studied her intransigent attitude. 'Fine!' he spat

out. 'That's fine by me. And I'm taking this gun
with me. I'm not going to be shot in the back by a
fool of a woman who doesn't know what's good for
her.'

He marched over to the Lagonda, tossed the gun
into the back seat, climbed in, slammed the door,
switched on the engine and, with an almighty burst
of acceleration, wheeled the car around and
screamed out on to the road.

'He's gone, Mum,' Robert stated unnecessarily.

'Yeah. We saved you, Mum,' Edmund said with
manly satisfaction.

Jackie slumped down on the steps and burst into
tears.

CHAPTER SIX

HOW could she have done such a dreadful thing? Geoff had told her, so many times, never, never, never to point a gun at anybody. Not for any reason. She hadn't meant to shoot. Not really. She had only meant to frighten him off. But giving such a terrible example to her sons! If Edmund had pulled the trigger ... The thought of the consequences made her shudder.

And Sunny King shielding her with his own body. Shielding her when she was the one at fault. So what thanks did she give him? Instead of backing him up when he had defused the dangerous situation she had screamed more abuse at him. He had every right to be angry. Every right. She was a total fool.

'Don't cry, Mum,' Robert pleaded. 'It's all right now.'

'It's not all right,' she sobbed. 'Everything's wrong. I haven't got the money to fix the place up, and you boys just go drifting off whenever you feel like it, and not telling me; and you could have got yourselves killed, and Edmund could have killed us this morning ...' More tears gushed from her eyes and she covered her face with her hands. Her whole body shook with sobs of despair.

Edmund sat down beside her and patted her

back. 'I wouldn't have shot you, Mum,' he assured her.

'And we wouldn't have gone abseiling without someone who knew all about it,' Robert explained. 'Trevor's had lots of experience.'

'He had no right to take you,' Jackie wailed. 'I told you no. Sunny King had no right to take it upon himself to ... to override my authority.'

'Well, er, you can't really blame him, Mum. We figured it was safe to go with Trevor so we sort of ... er gave Sunny the impression that you'd OK'd it.'

'Yeah, and he even tried to check with you but we made sure you'd gone shopping first,' Edmund supplied in the hope of making her feel better.

'We thought we'd get home earlier so you wouldn't notice, but we got stuck on a ledge for a while and ...'

'How could you?' Jackie burst out, absolutely beside herself. 'How could you tell such terrible lies? And I blamed Sunny King for letting you go.'

'They weren't real lies, Mum,' Edmund insisted.

'We just skirted around the whole truth. I mean we were bird-watching, too,' Robert argued with all the guile of a defence counsel. 'Please don't cry, Mum. We promise we'll do all the fixing up around the house for you. Just tell us what you want done.'

'Yeah. We'll make it up to you, Mum,' Edmund added soulfully. 'We'll be real good.'

Which left Jackie feeling even more defeated. The boys were getting beyond her control. Maybe they'd always been beyond her control. They just let her think she was in charge occasionally.

Robert took her hand. 'Come on in, Mum. Lie down for a while. I'll bring you a cup of coffee. You'll feel better soon.'

But Jackie didn't although the tears eventually dried up. She had wronged Sunny King, and Trevor Haines. But most especially Sunny King. Her only real grievance against him was the broken windscreen and he had more than redressed that wrong. She couldn't really take offence at the fact that he had considered her desirable, particularly since she hadn't exactly fought him off when he'd been kissing her. He wasn't to blame for what other people thought, either. And the new fence added value to her property.

So he was an arrogant show-off who thought the whole world was his personal oyster. That was no reason for her to shoot a gun at him. She was deeply ashamed of her unwarranted behaviour, even more ashamed as she kept remembering how he had protected her with his own body. He could have used her as a hostage for his own safety, but instead he had safeguarded her as best he could against any possibility of harm.

She owed him an apology, an abject apology; there was no getting away from that. The thought tormented her all day. The boys were model sons, Robert mowing all the grass, Edmund weeding the garden and making neat piles of all the rubbish lying around. After tea the boys settled down to a game of Monopoly, and Jackie could not put off her conscience any longer.

'I have to go and talk to Mr King,' she announced. 'I don't know how long I'll be. You're to go to bed at nine o'clock. And I mean nine o'clock.'

'Yes, Mum. Double promise,' Robert replied for both of them.

'We're tired from all that work anyway,' Edmund muttered, shaking the dice out on to the Monopoly board.

And so much for my authority, Jackie thought despondently. She drove the Daimler up the road to Sunny King's house. She couldn't keep his car any longer, not after what she had done. Somehow she and the boys would survive on what supplies she had in the house until her own car was returned.

Trevor Haines answered the doorbell and greeted her cheerily, obviously still ignorant of the morning's disastrous fiasco. But that didn't alleviate Jackie's inner misery. She had to confess to her own sons' perfidy.

'Mr Haines ...'

'Oh, please, call me Trevor. Sorry about being a bit late home with the boys yesterday, Mrs Mulholland. Hope you weren't worried.'

'Well, yes, I was. I'm afraid they misled you, Trevor. I had expressly forbidden them to go abseiling. Please don't think I blame you, as I'm aware of how ... how devious they can be.'

He went beetroot-red. 'I say, I'm most terribly sorry. Sunny did try to phone you, but ...'

'I know,' Jackie sighed. 'Robert and Edmund do tend to plan things very well. However, I'd appreciate it if you didn't take their word for anything from now on. Please check with me personally.'

'I most certainly will, Mrs Mulholland.'

Jackie took a deep breath. 'And now I'd like to speak to Mr King, if he's home.'

Trevor visibly dithered. 'Oh ... er ... I promise you it won't happen again, Mrs Mulholland.'

He really was very young. 'It has nothing to do with yesterday, Trevor,' she assured him. 'It's about a personal matter between Mr King and myself.'

'Aah!' He brightened. 'Please come in. I'm sure Sunny will be happy to see you.'

Jackie was not at all sure that Sunny King wouldn't order her out of his house, but she was grateful for Trevor Haines's innocent welcome. Grateful, also, that Sunny King hadn't seen fit to regale his secretary with details of this morning's madness.

'Sunny's watching an old movie down in the theatre,' Trevor informed her. 'I'll take you down.'

'Thank you,' Jackie murmured, and followed him with increasing nervousness.

The theatre was in darkness, apart from the big screen. Jackie took one look at the black and white picture of Ingrid Bergman and Humphrey Bogart and recognised the film as *Casablanca*. Which rather surprised her.

'Sunny ...' Trevor hissed.

The dark silhouette of Sunny King, slumped in one of the sofas on the far side of the room, made no move.

'Mrs Mulholland is here to see you,' Trevor announced confidently.

For a couple of nerve-racking moments Jackie thought Sunny King was going to ignore both of them. Then he leaned forward. The picture on the screen flicked off and an overhead light flicked on. He slowly rose to his feet, his face quite expressionless as he turned towards them.

'Thank you, Trevor,' he said coldly.

It was a dismissal, plain and simple, and Trevor needed no second hint. He closed the door quietly behind him, leaving Jackie to face Sunny King alone—which was what she wanted; but she felt hopelessly tongue-tied now that the moment of reckoning had come.

'Would you care for a glass of muscat?' Sunny King asked, waving to the bottle that stood on the low table in front of him.

'No. No, thank you,' she choked out.

He shrugged and sat down again, apparently having decided that any further gesture of hospitality would be wasted on her. He stared at the blank screen, completely ignoring her presence. His moody expression held a strong resemblance to that of her boys when they were sulking. Had she wounded his pride so deeply?

'*Casablanca* is one of the great movies,' she remarked, in an attempt to break the ice.

'Yes. It's about honour, and loyalty, and love,

and chivalry, and fair play.' He gave a feeling emphasis to every point.

A flush of shame burnt into Jackie's cheeks but he spoke on without giving her a chance to make her apology.

'Sentiments that aren't very fashionable these days, and yet they mean a great deal to me. But you don't see that, do you? To you I'm a rude and abhorrent troglodyte. A thing you shoot at.'

Oh, God! What had she done? Jackie had not known what to expect from him but somehow she had never considered that the irresponsible Sunny King had feelings that could be deeply hurt. Never had she felt so mean. So small. And she deserved every bit of his accusation.

He took a sip from his glass, then held it up to her in a mock toast. 'Perhaps you'll enlighten me as to why you've come to this whorehouse, Mrs Mulholland.'

Jackie swallowed hard to moisten her throat and forced the words out. 'I came to apologise, for myself and my sons.'

His eyes were hard, unforgiving, and he spoke with icy deliberation. 'Don't do that for your sons, Mrs Mulholland. As misguided as they were in their actions, I would have done precisely what they did in defence of my own mother. They love you deeply.'

His generosity threw her into confusion again. 'Then ... then I'm most terribly sorry for what I said and did. I ... I misunderstood things. But I know that's no excuse, and I'm not trying to excuse myself. I was wrong and stupid and . . . and I'm sorry.'

He took another mouthful of wine and his mouth curled sardonically over the glass. 'You've handed out quite a few insults, and I would like to know one thing, before I decide whether your apology is worth accepting or not.'

'And what's that?' Jackie asked, feeling more mortified than ever.

'Have you seen either one of the Dirk Vescum movies?'

The question surprised her until a few moments' reflection brought the realisation that he was fiercely proud of those movies and she had scorned and belittled them. 'No, I haven't,' she confessed miserably.

'So you condemn, unseen and unheard.'

The statement hung flatly in the air. It made Jackie feel that she had been a little unfair. She tried to explain. 'They do have a reputation for violence, and I abhor . . .' She stopped, too conscious of her own actions to defend herself.

Sunny King's smile was savagely ironic. 'There comes a time where violence can only be answered by violence, to prevent something worse happening,' he stated with pointed emphasis. 'However, that's something you have to make up your own mind about. If your apology is sincere, you'll give me a fair hearing.

'I . . . I don't understand.'

'I'll show you *Eye For An Eye* from start to finish.' He waved a careless invitation. 'Take a seat,

Mrs Mulholland. Any one will do. As far away
from me as you like.' He paused, eyeing her
cynically. 'Or you can stuff your apology into your
closed mind and walk out. Please yourself.'

She owed him that, Jackie acknowledged. Even
if she hated the film and all it represented, sitting
through it was a punishment she deserved. She
walked stiffly to the closest armchair and sat down.

He stared at her for a few long minutes, finished
his drink, walked to the back of the room and
opened a cupboard which contained many rows of
video recordings. He placed one in a machine,
walked back to the table, pressed a control which
switched off the overhead light, and lounged back
on the sofa he had occupied when she entered the
room.

The movie began. Jackie half-knew its story,
having been force-fed the more lurid details by
Robert and Edmund. It was a simple and hack-
neyed theme, set in an imaginary place at an
imaginary time. Dirk Vescum, the hero, refused to
fight invading aliens until his wife and family were
brutally killed by them. Dirk lost an eye before he
himself escaped. From then on he set out on a
vendetta of hatred and revenge until he met the
beautiful Alena, daughter of a renegade earthling,
who gave him a more balanced purpose for living.
Together they halted the alien challenge.

The story was trite, just as Jackie had anticipated. What she hadn't anticipated was the emotional manner in which Sunny King had developed it.
There were moments in the love-death scenes

which wrung her heart and almost moved her to tears. It wasn't overplayed. It was even under-stated, but the simplicity of every scene carried its emotional impact with tremendous force.

The action scenes were hectic, riveting with tension and explosive with one shock after another. The violence was certainly there, but it was always implied, never done in gruesome detail. The scenes were choreographed for action-shock and absol-utely gripping, despite the lack of costly special effects. The shoestring budget had not cramped the style, and Jackie marvelled at the ingenuity of the man who had got so much out of such limited means.

The development of the relationship between Dirk Vescum and Alena grew from initial antagon-ism to respect, and then to a reliance on each other's strengths, and not until the closing scene when the aliens had been stopped was there a look of understanding that suggested love might be possible between them.

No sex. Not even a kiss. Alena made a dry comment on the battle and Dirk Vescum looked at her and a smile slowly grew on his face, the first smile since his family had been killed. After a slight hesitation Alena smiled back, and that was the end, leaving the audience on a high note of emotional satisfaction.

Jackie was still caught up in it when the screen went blank and the overhead light glared down. Rather reluctantly she turned her head towards Sunny King. Hard blue eyes bored into her. One eyebrow rose in mocking enquiry.

'Crummy?'

'No, it wasn't crummy.' She searched her mind for an honest comment on what she had seen.

'Rotten?' he tossed at her.

'No.'

'Nothing but abhorrent violence?' he bored on.

Jackie suddenly realised that she had hurt more than his pride with her scathing criticism of his work. She had struck at the heart of the man, for only a man with a very feeling heart and great sensitivity could have made such a film.

'I'm sorry,' she said, her all-too-clever vocabulary completely failing her as she contemplated her dismal failure to give Sunny King his just due. 'It's a grand movie,' she admitted with new-born humility, and she wished with all her heart that he would smile at her as Dirk Vescum had smiled at Alena.

He didn't smile. Not one muscle in his face moved as he continued to stare at her, eyes as hard as diamonds. And she hated it. She wanted the twinkle back, the teasing laughter, anything but that total lack of reaction to her.

'I can now see why it has so much appeal, for such a broad spectrum of audience,' she offered in the hope that it would awaken a spark of interest.

Nothing.

She tried again. 'You chose a great cast. I can't imagine anyone playing the roles better.'

Still nothing.

Almost in desperation, Jackie cast around for

more words of praise, eventually hitting on Sunny King's contribution. 'There wasn't a dull moment. The direction was ... was brilliant.'

Not even that accolade cracked his stony façade.

Jackie felt as if she was being put through a wringer. Finally, limply, she said, 'It surprised me. I liked it. Very much.'

And that produced a response. 'Thank you.' He stood up, still with no softening of expression. 'I'm glad you didn't find it too much of an imposition on your time. If you're ready to go now, I'll see you safely home.'

His icy politeness chilled her to the bone. 'I ... I really am sorry,' she pressed anxiously as she rose to her feet.

'I now accept your apology, Mrs Mulholland.'

He held the door open for her and she really had no other option than to go. Sunny King was finished with her. His whole manner spelled that out with bitter clarity. And it hurt. The way he kept himself frigidly separated from her as they walked up the staircase hurt, too. Jackie told herself that she should have been relieved that any association with Sunny King was over, but she only felt miserable.

When they reached the front doors she couldn't bear it any longer. 'Please don't come any further with me, Mr King.' She held out the keys to the Daimler. 'Thank you for the use of your car. It's just outside near the garage. I won't be needing it any more. And it's only a short walk home. I'll be quite all right.'

He took the keys. 'I'll drive you home. It's dark, and I wish to be sure you get home safely.'

The cold statement brooked no argument. He accompanied her outside and held the passenger door of the Daimler open for her. Jackie slid into it, feeling smaller than ever. Sunny King's studied courtesy was like a slap in the face.

He drove her home at a sedate pace, with none of the squealing of tyres or burning of rubber that she associated with his driving. He slid the car to a quiet halt in her front yard and climbed out, apparently intent on seeing her to her door. For one crazy moment of hope Jackie thought he might suddenly change back into the Sunny King of old and take her in his arms, but he halted at the front steps and made no move to touch her. Jackie hesitated, torn by a dreadful feeling of having burnt bridges she might have liked to cross.

She sought for something to say, to keep him with her a little while longer, to throw some line across the chasm she had dug with her own blind stubbornness.

'Why . . . why did you come here this morning?' she asked, grasping at the one straw that came to mind.

'I wanted to give you something. It doesn't matter any more,' he replied, throwing back the same words she had used this morning. 'Good-night, Mrs Mulholland.'

She didn't have a leg to stand on. 'Goodnight, Mr King, and thank you for bringing me home,' she said, driven to match his politeness.

He nodded and turned away, striding off towards her gateway without even a glance at the Daimler.

'The car!' she called after him, too agitated by his leaving it not to make some protest.

He half-turned. 'I left the keys in it. Trevor will pick it up when he returns your car. You never know when you might need ready transport and I will not have you deprived of it because of a fault of mine. And before you stand on your pride, Mrs Mulholland, think of your children.'

Having delivered the one unanswerable argument, he turned his back on her and kept walking.

Jackie bit her lips and watched him, her heart sinking with every step he took away from her. She knew he wouldn't come back. Not ever again. And a terrible sense of loss closed in on her.

CHAPTER SEVEN

TREVOR HAINES returned Jackie's car to her the following Thursday. It gleamed like new. The bodywork had been polished and the inside of the car postively sparkled. Jackie felt intensely embarrassed as she accepted the keys from Trevor. The Daimler was sitting in the shed, gathering dust, and she hadn't thought to clean it.

'You didn't have to . . .' She faltered, conscious of sounding ungracious. 'I mean, it looks marvellous, but it wasn't necessary to . . .'

'Oh, the polish job,' Trevor chimed in brightly. 'Nothing to it. Sunny's orders, Mrs Mulholland. There were also a few rust spots that had to be cut out and you'll find the brakes more responsive than they were. You don't have to put your foot right to the floor any more. The brake lining was almost worn through, you know. Very dangerous. And most of the radiator hoses were perishing, so they've been replaced. Sunny had the engine tuned as well, and it's running like a charm.'

Jackie's mind was reeling over the cost of the repairs. She didn't have hundreds of dollars on hand. She had known the brakes needed checking when she put the car in for its next service, but she hadn't realised there was anything else in need of repair.

'I . . . I can't pay. Not until my next cheque

comes,' she said distractedly.

'No need to worry, Mrs Mulholland. It's all been paid for. Sunny said it was too dangerous for you and the kids and the general public, to have you driving around in a car like that. It worried him. I know it did.'

'But it was only supposed to be the windscreen,' she said helplessly. 'I can't accept all this from him.'

'Well, you take that up with Sunny, Mrs Mulholland, I just follow orders.'

She didn't know what to do. She couldn't imagine that Sunny King would take kindly to any argument from her over the matter. Or over any matter, when she came to think about it. On the other hand, she could go and thank him. In fact that was the least she could do in return for his thoughtful generosity.

Jackie had done a good deal of soul-searching over the last few days. The truth was, she had quite enjoyed the few confrontations with Sunny King. He had made her feel more intensely alive than she had felt for years. His high-handed manner had sharpened her wits and the way he had pursued her had been exciting, even though she had denied it to herself at the time. She wanted . . . Well, at least she wanted to be on friendly talking terms with him.

'Is Mr King at home?' she asked Trevor as she led him to the Daimler.

'No, he's gone. He suddenly decided to bring his schedule forward a bit. Shooting starts on the new movie next month. Lots of things to check before then. It's going to be the best of the lot, Sunny reckons,' Trevor informed her cheerfully.

Jackie's heart sank. 'When will he be back?' she asked, doing her best to project only casual interest.

Trevor shrugged. 'Probably four months or so. Depends on how things go. Bad weather can put you behind. Sunny doesn't do much studio stuff; most of it's on location and he lives with it night and day.'

So that was that, Jackie thought dispiritedly. She could forget Sunny King for four months at least. If she could.

'But there'll be Tom and Betty Willis looking after the place, so you don't have to worry about its being deserted,' Trevor added as he opened the door of the Daimler.

'Who are they?' Jackie asked curiously.

'Housekeeper and handyman. The couple Sunny hired to keep things running. They've got their own apartment at the back of the house.' He settled himself behind the wheel and turned on the ignition. 'I'll be joining Sunny tomorrow. Will you tell the boys goodbye for me?'

'Of course. Thanks, Trevor. And please thank Mr King for me and tell him . . . tell him I hope the movie goes well.' It was a small enough return for his generosity, but it was all she could think of.

'Sure thing, Mrs Mulholland. Bye now.'

She waved him off, then garaged her own car, over-conscious of looking after it now that it was in tip-top condition. It even smelled new. She lingered in the driver's seat, wondering why Sunny King had done all this for her. Trevor had said it was to make sure she would be safe on the road.

Which suggested that Sunny King really cared about her.

She had dismissed his extravagant speech about making her his woman and having children together. She had put that down to his desire to have sex with her. But maybe she was wrong. On Sunday night, when she had offered her apology, Sunny King had acted like a man who had been wounded very deeply. Was it simply ego, or did her opinion of him really matter?

Well, she had effectively killed any softness he had felt for her, Jackie thought with a heavy sigh. He had even put his schedule forward to get out of her way. Though that was probably reading too much into the situation. Maybe when he came back in four months' time ... Well, she would handle things differently, if he gave her the chance.

The summer holidays came to an end and the boys went back to school. Jackie secretly breathed a sigh of relief. School hours prevented them from getting up to too much mischief, although she had to admit they had been very good since the abseiling incident.

Jackie worked long hours at her pottery, intent on building up enough funds to have the house painted. On one of her selling trips to Parramatta she noticed that *Live By The Sword* was still playing at the Village Cinema, and, feeling curiously like a traitor to her own beliefs, she took time off to go and see it. As she sat in the theatre waiting for the main feature to start, she could not quell a lively sense of anticipation and for the first time really understood why the boys had argued so hard about being allowed to see the film.

It opened with the re-establishment of the relationship between Dirk Vescum and Alena, each being commander of a resistance force against the aliens. Without anything being said, it was apparent that Alena was in love with Dirk but he was keeping his distance, wary of committing himself to a deep emotional involvement.

On one of their patrols they rescued a band of half-wild children who were being rounded up by the aliens for experimental purposes. As Dirk led the children to safety, Alena and her two main lieutenants were ambushed. Alena was taken prisoner and her men killed. The main body of the story was the mission to rescue Alena and destroy the aliens' operations. Quite predictably Alena was about to be tortured when Dirk arrived on the scene and beheaded the alien scientists.

However predictable it was, the scene was electric and Jackie was on the edge of her seat, gnawing her knuckles until it was over. Even when Dirk had released Alena there was still no mushiness, as the boys would have put it, only a few moments of great tenderness which spoke volumes, and gave relief to the audience before the wild kids, who had accompanied Dirk, gave the warning that alien troops were arriving.

The battle was incomparable and, when Dirk and Alena finally won, the whole alien centre went up in a massive conflagration. The film ended with Dirk Vescum hugging Alena to him, understanding pulsing between them. However trite it was, Jackie had no doubt that everyone in the audience thought it was a marvellous ending.

In justice to Sunny King, Jackie felt she had to own up to the boys that she had gone to see the movie, and enjoyed seeing it. As she listened to their views over the dinner-table that night, she realised that it wasn't the violence that had enthralled them. Behind the appeal of exciting action was the strong sense of rightness, of good against evil, of feeling for others, of loyalty and bravery and honour and love: the principles and sentiments that Sunny King had told her he held dear.

An egocentric show-off he might be, and his early films were poor, but Jackie certainly couldn't write off the worth of what he was doing now. These last two films, where he had kept personal control on the product, were in another class entirely. They were good entertainment and carried a high level of morality and humanity which won her admiration and approval. There were obviously many dimensions to Sunny King that she had failed to appreciate.

'Well, now you'll come with us to the next Dirk Vescum movie,' Edmund said with happy enthusiasm.

'How do you know there will be a next one?' Jackie asked.

'Trevor told us, but he wouldn't tell us the story,' Robert put in a little plaintively.

'That's why they've gone away,' Edmund explained as if Jackie was singularly thick-headed. 'They're making the next Dirk Vescum movie.'

Over the next few weeks Jackie often wondered

how Sunny King would continue his story. She decided it probably didn't matter very much. He had that deft touch that could tug at the heart of any audience, involve them no matter what he was showing them. The pivotal strength of his movies was in the character: a hero who was human and vulnerable as well as having all the hero attributes, and a heroine one could respect and empathise with, not a stupid, clinging vine who always made silly mistakes, but someone who faced and coped with hard realities.

Jackie decided it was about time she faced up to a few hard realities. She called in a house painter to give her an estimate for painting the outside of the house. The figure he quoted horrified her, and when she questioned it he patiently explained that there was a lot of extra labour involved in scouring off the peeling paint before any new coats could be applied.

He left the itemised quotation with her. Jackie hadn't even realised that paint was so expensive. She could afford to buy that, but paying for the labour was out of the question. She and the boys would have to do it themselves, no matter how long it took them.

She borrowed a book on house painting from the library and purchased the necessary materials. At a round-table conference in the kitchen, she and the boys decided they could get one side of the house ready to paint after school hours, then paint it at the weekend. It didn't really matter how many weeks it took them. They all agreed it was better to start at the back of the house since they should be quite professional by the time they had worked around to the front.

As it turned out, they were all sick and tired of the job when they finally reached the front, but the gleaming white of the rest of the house made it look so bad in comparison that they resigned themselves to struggling on. Besides, the May vacation had begun and the boys didn't want the job hanging over their heads during the school holidays.

The tricky part was the high gable. The ladder wasn't long enough for Edmund or Robert to handle the work and Jackie herself had to reach up at full stretch. Edmund held the ladder steady while she stood on tip toe on the second-top rung.

The sudden screeching of tyres and subsequent hurtling of loose gravel almost made her teeter, and the bull-like roar of Sunny King did nothing to help her regain her balance.

'Get down! Get down from there this instant!'

For some inexplicable reason, Jackie began to shake. She leaned against the wall for support and fumbled a foot down on to the next rung of the ladder. She heard footsteps pounding across the front yard but she was too frightened to turn her head in case she fell.

'Just take it slow now, one rung at a time.' The roar had petered down into calm command. The voice came from just below her. 'If you fall I'll catch you,' it assured her.

'You startled me,' Jackie half-whimpered, then her voice gathered angry accusation as her foot found another rung and fear receded. 'I was all right until you had to do your rubber-burning act.

And you shouldn't have yelled at me like that.'

'Just shut up and get down. And why the hell are you painting the damned house? It's only fit for demolition.'

'It happens to be our home,' she yelled down at him, all her hackles rising at his high-handed denigration of their weeks of hard work.

He muttered something she couldn't quite catch but it was a mutter of some considerable feeling. And then she was back on the ground and glaring up at him and he was glaring down at her, and tears welled into Jackie's eyes because she had thought of him so much and this meeting was the very reverse of what she had planned.

'There's no point in talking to you, is there?' he growled and took the paint can from her. He flung a sharp look at Robert. 'Come over here and hold the ladder with Edmund. It'll probably shake more with my weight on it.'

He was half-way up the rungs before Jackie found her voice. 'What are you doing?' she asked stupidly.

'I'm going to paint the damned gable,' he threw at her in exasperation. 'If I don't do it, you're mad enough to go on with it as soon as my back is turned. And it's too dangerous for you.'

'But . . . but your good clothes!' For once he was conventionally dressed in a blue linen safari suit.

'I've got other clothes,' he snapped, and muttered something more about there being only one of her, thank God, whereupon he started slapping paint on to the old weatherboard with unnecessary vigour.

He was going to get paint spots all over him at that rate, Jackie thought, but held her tongue. It had finally filtered through that all his words and actions had been prompted by concern for her safety. And maybe he still cared about her.

She stood there, staring up at him, wondering how she could breach the wall of reserve between them. He was angry. There was anger in every stroke of the paint brush. Somehow she had to mollify that anger. She had caused it by frightening him and then snapping at him. She could at least try offering an olive branch, couldn't she? Even if he didn't take it, it showed good will on her part, which was more than she had ever shown him before.

He finished painting the top third of the gable and climbed down the ladder. 'Thanks, boys,' he muttered, releasing them from his command. Then he turned to Jackie, thrusting the paint tin and brush into her hands. 'Now you can get on with it without breaking your fool neck,' he gruffed dismissively.

'Thank you. It was very kind of you to help,' Jackie said meekly, not rising to his critical comment.

He shot her a sharp look and she offered him a smile. The flicker of surprise in the blue eyes encouraged her further. 'You can't get in the Lagonda with all that paint spattered on your hands and arms. Would you like to come in and clean up? It's an acrylic paint so it comes off with soap and water.'

He frowned down at his hands. 'Guess that

would be a good idea.' He lifted a carefully neutral look. 'If you don't mind.'

'Of course not. You're very welcome.' She led him in to the bathroom, very conscious of him following her down the hallway. The hairs on the back of her neck prickled. She was wearing the same shorts and T-shirt she had put on the night of his house-warming party. Did he still find her desirable?

There was no glimmer of it in his expression when she stood back to wave him into the bathroom, and, quite perversely, Jackie felt disappointed. She wanted something from him, something positive.

'I haven't had the chance to thank you for all the work you had done on my car,' she said brightly as she handed him a clean towel.

His mouth took on a sardonic curl. 'You don't owe me anything, Mrs Mulholland. I was looking after my own peace of mind.'

He was making it difficult. 'Nevertheless, I am very grateful to you. I ... I'm just going to make lunch. It's just sandwiches but if you'd like to join us ...' Oh, God! Of course he wouldn't want sandwiches, Jackie bemoaned to herself, a flush of hopeless embarrassment staining her cheeks. 'I'm not a very good housekeeper, and I suppose Mrs Willis is expecting you,' she mumbled in awkward excuse.

'No. Actually she isn't,' Sunny King said slowly.

Her eyes fluttered up to his in appeal and found a softening. 'Tomato and cheese?' she asked hopefully.

'Sounds fine.' And he smiled.

Jackie's heart flipped. She felt like skipping out to the kitchen but she forced herself to walk normally. 'Please overlook the mess. We wanted to get the painting finished so I'm a bit behind with the other work . . .' Her voice trailed away in shame at the weakness of the excuse.

'It's too much for you,' came the sympathetic comment.

'Not really. I manage most of the time,' she tossed back cheerfully, and noticed him looking around the living-room with interest.

He picked up the dinosaur on the coffee-table near the sofa and handled it curiously, a soft whimsical smile curving his mouth. He glanced up and caught her eyes on him. 'Yours?'

'Yes. It's a good selling line,' she added, glad that she hadn't brought up any llamas from the pottery shed.

'I like it. Has character,' he remarked, replacing it carefully.

'Thank you.'

He looked up and smiled again. 'You're very talented.'

'Only in a small way. Not in your class.'

His face stiffened and suspicion flashed into his eyes.

'I meant you reach millions of people with your art. I'm very small-time,' Jackie explained hastily.

He relaxed again and strolled over to her cassette collection on the shelves. 'Opera?' One eyebrow rose in quizzical disbelief. 'You like opera?'

'Love it.'

He shook his head. 'Can't stand it myself.'

The words zoomed out of her brain and almost poured of her tongue. She just clamped her mouth shut in time and, in case the urge to tell him what she thought of his ear-deafening taste in music became overwhelming, she quickly turned and moved into the kitchen.

Lots of people, most people, didn't like opera, she argued to herself as she banged a few plates down on the table and slammed the cutlery drawer. But it took someone of Sunny King's supreme arrogance to dismiss the greatest voices in the world and some of the greatest music ever written.

Jackie was aware that he had propped himself in the doorway and was watching her, but she didn't trust herself to look at him. She might be tempted to say something she might regret, although why on earth she wanted his good opinion she didn't know. They were poles apart in taste . . . nothing in common at all. They couldn't even talk for five minutes without her wanting to snap at him.

'I don't mind your liking opera though,' he declared benevolently.

Well, thank you very much, Jacke bristled. How kind of him to grant her his seal of approval! She couldn't resist a couple of shots at him. 'You should try it sometime. Open your mind to it,' she suggested sweetly.

'I have. Tried it I mean. Didn't do anything for me. But maybe I need you to show me how to enjoy it. I like your liking it. It kind of suits you.'

She felt a twinge of shame. He was being more tolerant than she was. She quelled her irritation and looked up into eyes that wanted her to like him. Shame forced a smile. 'Why do you think it suits me?' she asked, projecting light interest into her voice.

His grin held relief. 'Oh, I guess it's because you have that kind of high-tone class.'

The compliment brought a warm flush of pleasure to her cheeks even as she gave a rueful laugh. 'I don't know how you can say that after what I did to you. I was terribly wrong.'

'Trevor told me that the boys lied about having your permission to go abseiling,' he said quietly. 'I guess you were worried sick.'

He was excusing her! Jackie's flush grew painful with guilt. 'I didn't even give you the chance to tell me why you had come over that morning,' she said apologetically.

'It was just to offer you and the boys the use of the pool whenever you liked. I thought ...' He shook his head and quickly added, 'Let's forget it. Can I help you with the sandwiches? I could butter the bread.'

She needed time to regain her composure. 'No. I ... I can handle it. Would you call the boys in to wash their hands?'

'Sure,' he said good-naturedly, and went off to do her bidding.

Jackie heaved a sigh to relieve her pent-up emotion, then quickly busied herself with slicing tomatoes. If Sunny King could overlook her faults, surely she could overlook his? He was her neighbour and life would be much more pleasant if she could be friends with him. Basically he was a good, kind person and she could not look down her nose at those qualities, no matter what else he might do that irritated her.

The boys came in, obviously pleased about this apparent truce between their mother and Sunny King, and all too ready to take advantage of it.

'Have you finished the movie, Sunny?' Robert asked eagerly.

'Finished shooting it. Still some work to be done on it though.'

'When will it be coming out in the cinemas?' Edmund pressed.

'Not for a while. I won't release it until I'm fully satisfied with it.'

'Is it as good as the last?'

Pleasure rippled through Sunny King's laughter. 'I hope it's better.'

'Mum's going to come with us to see it,' Robert said in the manner of delivering the ultimate accolade to Sunny King's work.

The blue eyes shot her a questioning look.

'Yeah,' Edmund chimed in. 'She went and saw *Live By The Sword* and thought it was great. Didn't you, Mum?'

Which put her fairly and squarely on the spot, fixed by three pairs of demanding eyes. 'I enjoyed it very much,' she said lightly, aware of a self-conscious flush creeping up her neck again. She shoved a plate of sandwiches into the centre of the table to distract their attention. 'Help yourselves,' she invited, and turned away to put the electric kettle on.

'Have you put the wild kids into this one?' Robert asked.

'No. It's a completely new adventure.'

'Aw,' said Edmund, disappointed. 'I thought they were terrific.'

The whole conversation over lunch revolved around the Dirk Vescum movies and Jackie was not allowed to stand back from it. The boys continually involved her, quoting what she had said about them, forcing her into admissions. And with each admission, Sunny King's pleasure glowed a little brighter until he was fairly beaming at her, and Jackie was growing increasingly warmer under his sparkling gaze.

'I think it's time we got back to work,' she finally declared, needing some activity fast. Sunny King was eating her up with his eyes and she was terribly aware of a squirmish anticipation in herself. She had this wild fantasy of him reaching over the table for her, pulling her across it and kissing her out of her mind. And the dreadful part was, it excited her.

The boys groaned. 'Couldn't we have the rest of the day off, Mum?' Robert begged.

'We've been working like slaves,' Edmund said hopefully.

'There's not much of this first coat left to do. Let's get it finished,' Jackie insisted, and leapt up to gather the plates and put them in the sink. 'Come on now,' she said more emphatically as they lingered at the table.

Sunny stood up. 'Better do as your mother says.' He smiled at her. 'Thanks for the lunch. I really enjoyed it.'

'You're welcome,' she said as lightly as she could, and shepherded them all out to the veranda before she made an absolute fool of herself.

'I'm expecting some business calls so I have to go,' Sunny said with obvious reluctance, 'but I'll come back tomorrow and put a second coat of paint on that high part for you.'

'I ... I really can do it myself,' Jackie half-protested, a little frightened by the strength of her physical response to him. She realised now that she had been fooling herself about their becoming friends. The sexual chemistry between them would always get in the way, forcing a development she wasn't sure she could cope with.

His hand closed around her wrist in sharp emphasis. 'But you're not to do it,' he said, frowning at her. 'It's not safe.' His gaze stabbed at the boys. 'Robert, Edmund, you're not to let your mother paint the top of that gable. Agreed?'

'OK, Sunny,' Robert agreed cheerfully. 'Can Edmund and I have a ride in the Lagonda? Just along the road to your place? We'll be right back, Mum.'

Sunny King raised his eyebrows at her and she nodded, her voice completely strangled by the sensation being aroused by his hand stroking down her arm and across her wrist. Her pulse was reacting in leaps and bounds. He smiled again at her and she wondered if he knew what he was doing to her.

'See you tomorrow then,' he said in soft promise, and let her go.

The boys streaked off to get into the Lagonda

and he followed them. Jackie watched in dismay as the car roared off down the road with the usual scattering of gravel. Sunny King was just a big kid himself, lapping up praise, showing off, wanting to get his own way all the time. She was mad to have anything to do with him. It couldn't lead anywhere good.

But tomorrow couldn't come fast enough.

CHAPTER EIGHT

THE boys returned quite promptly from their ride with Sunny King and the first coat of paint was completed by mid-afternoon. Having earned their freedom, Robert and Edmund quickly disappeared on their own business. Jackie briefly wondered what they were up to, but she heard their voices in their bedroom and didn't think any more about it. There were other, more pressing matters on her mind.

She had a shower and washed her hair, then took a critical appraisal of herself in the mirror above the wash basin. She had always considered her breasts a bit on the large side, not exactly uncomfortable but more prominent than she liked. But they weren't sagging. Yet. She supposed that pummelling clay kept up the muscle tone.

She sighed over her thickened waist. Child-bearing did that to you, she told herself. It was no use expecting to look like a young girl ever again, but she didn't look too bad, considering that she had passed thirty. There were a couple of cellulite dimples on her bottom but she had always been over-endowed in that area, and he had said he liked cheeky bottoms.

He! She caught herself up on that word and dragged in a deep breath. Was she really going to take the plunge and have an affair with Sunny King? That was all it could possibly be. They simply weren't compatible enough to live together in any kind of harmony. It couldn't last.

And what was she going to do when it was over? Jackie demanded of the feverish anticipation in her mirrored eyes.

Worry about that when it happens, came the voice of galloping temptation.

And what about the effect on Robert and Edmund? conscience rumbled.

Be discreet.

Huh! Sunny King wouldn't know the meaning of the word 'discreet'! He'd most likely want to flaunt his success with her in front of the whole world, just as he flaunted all his other successes in every way possible.

Jackie grabbed a bath towel, wrapped it around her treacherous body and scooted off into her bedroom to get dressed. Nudity was not conducive to sane reasoning. It was definitely insane to be considering an affair with Sunny King. Yet she definitely—well, not definitely ... But it was a terrible temptation. She had never felt like this before. With Geoff it had been more romantic. Not so ... so compelling.

She tidied up the living-room, ironed the boys' school clothes, and tried to think sensible thoughts. Without much success. She cooked tea and called the boys out of their room, hoping that their conversation would lift her mind off Sunny King.

It didn't. They were full of impressive facts about the Lagonda.

Having disposed of the hamburgers and chips Jackie had cooked, they decided to take their plates of ice-cream into the living-room so that they could watch *The Depths Of Space—How To Survive* on television. Jackie hoped it would be interesting enough to take her mind off Sunny King.

Suddenly a blinding white light flashed into the hallway. A loud sizzle like the sound of frying meat came from the boys' bedroom.

'Aw gee!' Edmund groaned. 'It's all gone up at once.'

For a moment Jackie was too stunned to move. Then she was off her chair and running down the hallway. Even before she reached the boys' door she could see fingers of flame leaping along the carpet. She turned and ran back to the kitchen for a bucket of water.

'What were you doing in your bedroom?' she screamed at the boys.

'Only a chemistry experiment,' Robert muttered, climbing to his feet to inspect the damage.

'Stay out of my way!' Jackie screeched across the kitchen counter.

Water slapped over the brim of the bucket. She dragged it out of the sink and raced for the hallway, uncaring of spillage. The heat emanating from the boys' room was suffocating. She threw the water at the door. Thick clouds of smoke rolled out, making her cough and stinging her eyes. The smell of ammonia assailed her nostrils.

Horror gripped her heart as she forced herself to look into the room. The water had had no appreciable effect upon the centre of the fire and it was already leaping up the curtains, licking around the window sill. She had no hope of stopping it. Any attempt to save the house was a waste of time. She fled back to the boys.

'Get out!' she yelled. 'Get outside immediately!'

The crackling of the old wood behind her was evidence enough of what was happening, but the boys just stood there, white-faced and shaken, staring mutely at their frantic mother. With an almighty roar the flames tore down the hallway. Jackie grabbed the boys' hands and pulled them towards the back door, her only thought being to get them to safety. The increasing roar of the fire taking hold heightened her terror. The old wood was burning like a tinder-box. Within a minute they'd be engulfed in flames.

'Run! Run for your lives!' she cried, shoving the boys ahead of her as they reached the back door.

They pelted down the yard with Jackie hard on their heels. At what she judged to be a reasonably safe distance she stopped and turned to see flames exploding out of the windows and sweeping up the newly painted walls. She swung on Robert who was panting beside her.

'What chemistry experiment were you carrying out?' she demanded.

He tore his horrified gaze from the burning house and took a frightened gulp. 'We were lighting magnesium ribbon with a candle ... and

... and then you called us out to tea and ... and then ... something must have happened.'

'Where did you get the magnesium ribbon from?' Jackie asked in bewilderment.

'I ... er ... I nicked it from the science lab at school,' he confessed miserably.

'Oh, Robert!' She did not have the heart to say more but the sad despair in her voice reached him far more deeply than anything else she might have said.

He looked up at her with tears in his eyes and for once he had no comeback, no excuse, no defence.

'It wasn't all his fault,' Edmund cried. 'I asked him. I wanted to see. It's my fault, too. But we didn't mean it to blow up, Mum.' The tearful plea begged her forgiveness.

She automatically cuddled them both in comfort. 'I know,' she sighed. 'I know you didn't mean it.' With bleak, grieving eyes she looked back at the flaming pyre of all their possessions. Sparks were flying off the roof in the direction of the shed.

'The car!' she choked. 'We've got to save the car!' Panic drove her feet the thirty metres to the shed as she frantically yelled instructions. 'Edmund, you steer it. Robert, help me push it.' The car key was in the house. No hope of getting it. The boys raced to do her bidding.

The damned car wouldn't budge. A sob of frustration broke from Jackie's throat. She wasn't thinking clearly; the car was still in gear. Frantically she ran around to the passenger side and whipped the gear stick into neutral.

'Push when I tell you, Robert,' she cried, running back to the nearest headlight. 'Now!'

Slowly the car moved backwards. It was halfway out of the garage when the back tyres hit the slight hump on the driveway. No matter how hard they tried, they couldn't push the car beyond that hump. Tears welled into Jackie's eyes. They were going to lose everything. And she couldn't risk keeping the boys here any longer. Sparks were flying everywhere. They had to leave. Get back to safety. A car wasn't worth endangering their lives.

'Jackie! Jackie!'

Never had she been so pleased to hear Sunny King's bull-like roar. She stumbled out of the garage, exhausted from the efforts to shift the car. 'We're here!' she cried. 'We need help! We can't move it any further.'

No sooner had she finished speaking than Sunny King was there, flinging her away from the shed. 'Get your shoulder into it, Trevor!' he yelled. 'Edmund's inside. Push, Robert!'

The car literally jumped over the hump and was quickly moved to a safe distance. Before Jackie could pick herself up Sunny King was back, sweeping her into his arms and carrying her away from the shed. She glanced back over his shoulder. The whole house was totally ablaze and, with a sudden whoosh, the shed they had just left caught fire.

She groaned at the nearness of their escape and Sunny King stopped in his stride and gentled his hold on her. 'Are you hurt?' he asked anxiously.

'Did you get burnt anywhere?' He carefully lowered her feet to the ground so he could examine her for injury.

'No, I'm all right,' she assured him, but she felt faint and was glad of his support when his arms came around her and pulled her against him. She nestled her head on his shoulder, too desolated by the disaster around her to do anything but accept the comfort he offered.

It was all gone, all that she had struggled and saved for over the years, everything she and the boys had owned, all the mementoes of their lives, turning to ashes in front of her eyes. All they had left were the clothes they stood up in. And the car. The stupid car that had almost cost them their lives.

'Jackie, I swear to God I had nothing to do with this. I know I said the house was only fit for demolition, but not this way. You must believe me!'

The agonised words jabbed into her ear, forcing her head up. She looked into eyes that were dark pools of torment. Her brain was sluggish, but instinct told her how deeply he cared that she did not lay this at his door. 'I know you had nothing to with it, and I know you wouldn't ever wittingly do anything to harm anyone,' she answered softly.

He heaved a great sigh and hugged her even more tightly. 'I thought you were in there. I thought ... Thank God you got out in time!' he muttered feverishly, his mouth moving over her hair in passionate relief.

Jackie felt too numb to care about anything until there was another explosive crack and the pottery shed burst into flame. A hoarse cry of despair burst from her throat at the realisation that the means of their livelihood was disintegrating before her eyes. Not only was the past gone, but any foothold on the future, too.

'Don't worry. I'll look after you. It'll be all right,' Sunny crooned to her over and over again as she laid her head on his shoulder and wept inconsolable tears.

'It's all my fault,' Robert said miserably.

'And mine,' Edmund sniffed.

'Trevor, take the boys home. Get Betty Willis to look after them.'

'No. We're staying with Mum,' Robert insisted, a catch of tearful emotion in his voice.

'Boys, your mother's got enough grief at the moment,' Sunny explained gently. 'Don't give her any more. Go with Trevor so she'll know you're safe. I'll bring her home with me when she's ready.'

'I'm sorry, Mum,' Robert choked out, pressing his head against her back for a brief moment.

'Me, too,' Edmund sobbed.

Jackie lifted her head to say something to them but Trevor was already leading them away and she felt too drained to resist Sunny's orders.

Cars began pulling up at the gateway, neighbours who had seen the fire and come to see if they could be of any help. It was all too evident that nothing could be saved, but they stayed on, morbidly fascinated by the disaster. Sunny kept his arm around Jackie, supporting her through the whole ordeal; answering questions, issuing orders, taking care of every contingency.

The Bushfire Brigade eventually arrived and set about putting the fire out. By the time they had finished there were only a few blackened beams left standing and a heap of debris on the ground. Beyond the smoking remains of the house stood the old brick kiln, a lone sentinel to what had once been a home.

The firemen declared the area safe and departed. The neighbours straggled off home, one by one taking sympathetic leave of Jackie. She stood there within the protective circle of Sunny King's arm, nodding dumbly to their meaningless words.

Even when they were all gone she did not move. This was her place, her home, and she stood mourning over it in hopeless grief, barely aware of the man beside her. The heat from the fire gradually dissipated on the cool night air. She began to shiver.

'Time to go,' Sunny King said gently.

She looked up at him with bleak, empty eyes. 'I have nowhere to go.'

'Yes, you have. My house is yours for as long as you want.'

She shook her head, feeling too bereft to even consider what he was offering her.

He tenderly cupped her face in his hands and forced her to meet his steady gaze. 'There are no strings attached, Jackie. Please come with me.'

A belated appreciation of the kindness and

sensitivity he had shown her tonight drove a stab of shame into her numb heart. 'Thank you for all you've done.'

His hands dropped to her upper arms, rubbing warmth into them. He spoke with urgent intensity. 'Jackie, you're in a state of shock. You must come with me. The boys are over there waiting for you. There's nothing more you can do here.'

'Yes. All right,' she got out stiffly.

His arm came around her waist, drawing her along with him as he headed towards the gateway. 'Don't worry about anything. I'll take care of you and the boys,' he assured her.

A man was standing by the Daimler, holding the back door open for them. 'The missus has got your boys safely tucked up in bed, Mrs Mulholland,' he said stoutly.

'This is Tom Willis, Jackie,' Sunny murmured.

'Thank you.' She couldn't thing of anything else to say.

Sunny bundled her into the back seat and got in after her. Tom Willis drove the Daimler down the road. Jackie felt too weary to protest when Sunny lifted her out of the car and carried her into his house. It was much easier to let herself be cradled in his arms and rest her head against his shoulder.

A middle-aged woman met them in the foyer. 'I put the electric blanket on in the turret room. I thought ...'

'That's fine. This is Betty Willis, Jackie.'

'Thank you,' she mumbled.

'Poor girl,' the housekeeper clucked. 'I put out

one of my nighties for her.'

'Good of you,' Sunny King approved. 'A cup of sweet tea, I think, Betty. And a couple of sleeping tablets.'

He took Jackie into the turret room, sat her down on the tiger bed and began to undress her. She weakly caught at his hand as his fingers flicked open the second button on her blouse.

The blue eyes bored straight into hers. 'It's all right,' he said; direct, unequivocal, nothing but help intended.

It was all right, Jackie thought vaguely. Modesty didn't matter. He had seen her before. He gently removed her blouse, slid a voluminous flannelette nightie over her head and poked her arms into the sleeves. He unbuckled her sandals and drew them off the feet, then propped her up to take off her skirt and briefs, his actions as impersonal as that of a nurse.

'Want to go to the bathroom?'

She nodded and he showed her into an en suite bathroom. She couldn't seem to manage very well. She was still at the wash basin trying to soap her hands when Sunny entered. He wiped her hands dry, picked her up and put her to bed, tucking the tiger quilt around her.

Mrs Willis came in carrying a tray. Jackie took a few sips of tea, automatically swallowed the tablets that were handed to her, then gratefully sank back down on the pillows. The bed was soft and warm. It felt good.

She had no recollection of going to sleep, nor of

dreaming, but she woke sometime during the night hearing her own voice screaming, 'Run! Run!' And another voice soothed, 'They're safe. You're all safe. You can relax. Go back to sleep.' The comfort of arms holding her safe lulled the nameless fear and it was light when she woke again.

For a few moments she felt totally disorientated. The tiger print on the tent-like curtaining brought memory flooding back. She stifled a groan, burying her face in the pillow, and only with that movement did she become aware of the arm beneath it, underneath her pillow. Slowly, carefully, with the minimum of disturbance to the bed, she turned around and stared at the man beside her.

He was still asleep, his face innocently boyish in repose, despite the golden beard. A crumpled collarless shirt clothed the top half of his body. She couldn't remember what he had worn last night but she guessed that he hadn't undressed, that he hadn't moved from her side all night. She remembered the comfort of arms cradling her when she had wakened in fear and knew he had stayed for her sake, ready to give whatever she needed. She felt humbled by all he had done for her.

'My house is yours for as long as you want.' She remembered those words. And the others, 'no strings attached'. She was sure that he had meant them sincerely at the time, but she could not fool herself into thinking that nothing would happen between them if she stayed. The attraction was there, too strong for her to resist for very long, and she couldn't possibly feel right about having an affair with him under these circumstances.

Where could she go? Her parents would take her in but that would only be under sufferance on both sides. They had more or less washed their hands of her when she had married Geoff instead of going on with the higher education they had planned for her. They would hate the disruption to their lives; she would hate depending on them. The boys would hate it even worse, being cooped up in a city town-house with no garden at all to play in.

She wondered how long it took for insurance to come through, if it was possible to get an immediate loan on the strength of it. Not that the insurance would be all that much. Not enough to build another house at today's prices. She would probably have to rent something until she could sell the land. Just the thought of doing that wrenched her heart.

She didn't want to leave here. And the truth of the matter was, she didn't want to leave Sunny King either. She didn't understand why he caused her to react so strongly—both emotionally and physically—infuriating her one minute then arousing a wild desire in her the next. Either way, she couldn't just shrug him off. He was a force she couldn't ignore or forget, and he certainly wasn't all bad, as she had first thought.

So, he liked to live in the grand manner; there was also a grandeur of soul in him that appealed to her. He valued the things she valued or he could not have created those Dirk Vescum movies. He was kind and generous, and the arrogance that she had scorned ... well, maybe he had a right to be arrogant. What other person had done what he had done?

A smile tugged at her mouth. Sunny King, the last of the great romantics. That could very well be true, she thought with a sudden will of affection, and on impulse she leaned over and kissed him.

His eyes suddenly opened, locking instantly on to hers, watchful, searching, wary. 'I thought I felt the touch of an angel,' he murmured, his voice soft and seductively musical.

The fanciful words brought a self-conscious flush to her cheeks. 'I'm sorry. I didn't mean to wake you. I shouldn't have done that.'

'As long as you're my guest you can do what you like and no harm will ever come to you.'

It was a grand gesture, so typical of the man she now knew him to be. Jackie had to smile. 'You really are a marvellous person,' she said in all sincerity. He would undoubtedly give her the shirt off his back if he thought she needed it.

'On the other hand, if you smile at me like that, I'm liable to forget my good intentions,' he warned, relief and pleasure taking any threat out of the words.

Nevertheless, Jackie dropped back on to her pillow, all too aware that now was not the time to be tempting fate. He did not follow her, except with his eyes. They were still searching hers but now with a sparkle of hope in them.

'I want you to stay with me, Jackie. Will you give it a chance?'

Live with him, he meant. In the fullest sense of the word.

'On any terms you like,' he corrected quickly. 'Just stay with me.'

But the desire for her was there in the urgency of his voice. She couldn't ignore it. 'Can I be brutally frank with you?' she asked softly.

'I'd rather you be honest,' he answered without hesitation.

Every bit of reasonable common sense she possessed told her to point out that their personalities were too different, that they would be clashing all the time, and she couldn't subject her children to the kind of tension which would inevitably develop between them if they lived together. But the look in his eyes curled around her heart, smothering common sense and forcing other words on to her tongue.

'I want to make love with you.'

The forthright admission sparked an immediate gleam of anticipation in the compelling blue eyes, and Jackie rushed out more words, panicking a little at the impulsive decision she had made. 'Not today. Today there's too much else on my mind and it wouldn't be right. But sometime, when it is right, I'm going to do that. I guess I've wanted it all along. Certainly I did last night before the fire broke out.'

'What about afterwards, Jackie?' Concern drew his eyebrows together. 'Would we still be friends or would you be bored? Disappointed?'

'I honestly don't know.' She saw the hurt her

admission gave him and quickly added, 'But I wouldn't stay here with you unless I felt there was hope for both of us . . . for being happy together.'

His face relaxed into a smile. 'You are a very remarkable woman, Jackie Mulholland.'

Jackie thought she was probably off her brain but right now she didn't care. She smiled back at him. 'And you're a very remarkable man, Mr King.'

Their smiles grew warmer with mutual satisfaction, building a sense of intimacy that had nothing to do with touching.

'What's your real name?' Jackie asked quietly. 'It can't possibly be Sunny.'

His eyebrows rose in quizzical amusement. 'You don't like Sunny?'

She wrinkled her nose at him. 'Tell me the truth.'

'Aloysius Reginald King. Take your pick,' he invited with an open grin.

'You're not kidding me?'

'That's what's on my birth certificate. I can show it to you.'

She sighed. 'I guess I'll get used to Sunny.'

He gathered her up and pulled her over his chest, his eyes laughing up at her. 'It's how you make me feel, all bright and warm and sparkly.'

Which was how she was feeling, too, despite having lost everything she had ever owned. 'I'd better get up and see to the boys.'

'See to a lot of things,' he agreed happily. He kissed her on the nose, rolled her back to her pillow, tossed the bedclothes aside and fairly leapt to his feet in a burst of energy. 'I must get in touch with my architect straight away,' he announced. 'Have to start building again.'

'Building what?' she asked, feeling an apprehensive tingle in her spine. 'Sunny, I can't afford to ...'

'I'm not going to have you bored. We're going to build the best pottery workroom that any potter ever had. Every kind of kiln ...'

'No. No!'

'Then the house ...'

'Stop it, Sunny! You're taking over again.'

It was as if he hadn't heard her. '... We'll build it on a scale that will leave the world bemused,' he burbled on, totally enthralled with his own ideas.

'Stop thinking like that at once!' Jackie shrilled at him. 'I can't afford it! I can't!'

'Don't worry about money. I've got money to burn,' he declared happily. 'Who's the best architect?'

'We don't need ...'

'Joern Utzon! He designed the Sydney Opera House. That's who we'll get. I'll build you the house of your dreams. Everything you've ever ...'

'There's nothing wrong with this house!' she cried in panicky protest.

He frowned at her. 'You don't like it. You said it was dreadful.' The frown disappeared into blissful enthusiasm. 'We'll have the ultimate in elegance, the ...'

'I like this house!' Jackie insisted wildly. 'I love it. It's a great house.'

'Stop interrupting me. I have this vision . . .'

'Sunny!'

'All those house plans are still in my study.' Excitement beamed at her. 'I'll be right back with your clothes. Betty took them off to launder them last night. Ah, we're going to have a marvellous day,' he threw at her exultantly and was out of the door before Jackie could find any retort at all.

She slumped back on her pillow and rolled her eyes. Well, she'd made her bed. This was it. It wasn't as if she hadn't known that Sunny King was uncontrollably mad. Besides, it might turn out to be marvellous. All she had to do was bend a little. Maybe a lot. But if Sunny King was mad, it was in a beautiful, beautiful way. And she had no regrets at all about her decision. Not yet anyway.

CHAPTER NINE

WELL, she certainly hadn't been bored, Jackie reflected, as she drove her old Datsun towards St Alban's. Frustrated, exasperated, and debilitated by Sunny's unstoppable dynamism, yes ... but never bored.

Sometimes she thought she was living with a brick wall, and, no matter how much she battered her head against it, it seemed impervious. Then, suddenly, unpredictably, it gave way, only to reappear from another direction.

Like the clothes. She had won the battle of the clothes and paid for them herself, establishing some independence from Sunny's compulsive generosity. She hadn't been able to buy much, apart from re-fitting the boys for school and a few necessary items for herself, but it was enough to go on with until the money came through from the insurance. However, while she was buying clothes, Sunny was off buying compact discs of all the greatest operas ever recorded. Hundreds and hundreds of dollars worth of music, just for her.

'Please send them back,' she had begged.

'Everyone's entitled to enjoy their own kind of music. Food for the soul. Isn't that what they say? I wouldn't be looking after you properly if you didn't have food for your soul,' was the solemn reply.

'Sunny, I don't want you spending a lot of money on me,' she had insisted.

He had looked hurt. 'But that's my pleasure.'

She had dug her toes in. 'I won't play them. You have to send them back.'

'No. I'm not going to have you getting bored,' was his final line on the argument and the box of discs was still sitting in her room.

Then came the trail-bikes for Robert and Edmund. It had been very hard to argue with Sunny in the face of the boys' delirious joy, but she had tried. 'Boys have to have trail-bikes,' he had growled. 'Otherwise they're not boys.'

It didn't matter how much she protested, somehow he defeated her. How did one fight against a man whose pleasure was in giving pleasure? His eyes sparkled excitement and happiness at her and she ended up weak-kneed. And of course, the boys thought he was marvellous. Which he was.

But Jackie didn't like the feeling of being steamrollered all the time. The years of careful planning and budgeting had instilled a caution in her that was continually appalled by Sunny's extravagance. She wasn't even sure that he had shelved the idea of designing her a new house, although she had done her best to convince him that she couldn't possibly afford it. He didn't seem to understand that concept at all.

Or didn't want to. He refused to accept any

contribution from her towards their keep and Jackie was beginning to feel quite stressed by the situation. She couldn't just stay on indefinitely, accepting his largesse. On the other hand, she didn't want to leave him. She wished she had her old house back, then she could still enjoy a relationship with him without feeling so damned beholden to him.

There was not one day that passed that Sunny didn't put her in some emotional dilemma. Like this morning. 'Since you're only going into the city to finalise this insurance business, and you don't like me buying you things, I think I'll stay at home,' he had declared, but Jackie was accustomed to spotting evasion on Robert's and Edmund's faces, and she saw that same shiftiness on Sunny's.

'Oh? What are you going to do here?' she had asked, pretending to be disappointed.

Sunny had a moment's pause, then his face had lit up. 'Robert and Edmund need to be taught the finer points of safe riding on their trail-bikes.'

'You? Teach them safe riding?' she had choked. It was madness. Sunny was worse than the boys.

'Yes. Things like how to ride out of a skid and what to do if you're going to fall. Very important to know things like that. Save them from injury.'

How could she argue against that? But if they were still all in one piece by the time she arrived back, it would be the world's eighth wonder. And Sunny had looked overly pleased with her compliance. He really was worse than the boys. She couldn't trust him out of her sight not to get up to some kind of mischief.

Jackie came over the crest of the last hill on the home stretch and Sunny's latest bit of mischief was right in front of her eyes. She slammed on the brakes, parked on the side of the road, and gaped at the biggest bulldozer she had ever seen. It was making a last sweep through the remnants of her house. The old brick kiln was gone. A traxcavator was shovelling up the last of the blackened bricks and dumping them into the back of a waiting truck. Jackie got out of the car and walked over to the new fence in a daze.

The fence is the first to go . . .

Then the kiln and the ramshackle sheds . . .

Then the house . . .

And then you. I'm going to take you under my wing and give you all you deserve.

Those had been Sunny's words, as well as she could remember them, and here it was . . . all done . . . except the final surrender from her. And that was only a matter of time now that she was living under his roof. Sunny had not pressured her to go to bed with him. He seemed content to wait until she was ready, and Jackie knew in her heart that it was inevitable. In fact, the closer the inevitable came, the more appeal it seemed to have.

With a strange bittersweet sadness, Jackie had to acknowledge that Sunny had been right about her old home messing up his view. Now that everything had been razed to the ground, she could see that the area was much prettier with just country-side all around Sunny's house. Even his monstrosity of a house seemed right, its turrets poking up to the sky like a small medieval castle, lord and master of all it surveyed.

A little smile played around her mouth. It was crazy but she was beginning to like Sunny's house. She no longer thought of her tiger-room as grotesque. It was like a sumptuous, romantic fantasy and she enjoyed waking up in it, luxuriating in the sensual opulence of all the furnishings. It was the kind of room that no one but Sunny King would dare to have, but wasn't it what everyone secretly wished to experience at least once in a lifetime?

And really, the whole house was like that. Like Sunny himself. Grandeur run riot. Totally uninhibited. And it was fun. Jackie even had to admit to occasionally pretending she was one of those old-time movie actresses making a grand entrance as she walked down the curved staircase.

But is wasn't her home, and she had to start making some definite plan about the future. The house insurance was not enough to build again. Maybe if she took from the capital of Geoff's life insurance ... But if she did that, could she make enough pottery for them to live on? The sensible thing to do would be to sell the land, which she knew would fetch a high price. Except that that meant moving away.

She climbed back into her car and drove on up to Sunny's driveway, having resolved nothing. As she entered the house, Sunny came bounding up the staircase from his study, his expression an odd mixture of anxiety and pleasurable anticipation. 'I've got something to show you!' he exclaimed, somewhat unnecessarily, his eyes darting warily over her expression.

'I see you got rid of the eyesore,' she said in dry resignation.

'It was dangerous, Jackie,' he said slowly, measuring her attitude as he spoke. 'The boys were poking around over there the other day. I thought I'd better send the bulldozer in. Save them from any harm.'

She had to smile. If there was a way around anything she was sure Sunny would find it. 'There couldn't be a better reason than that,' she said with warm approval.

Surprise and relief chased over his face. 'You're not mad with me?'

'You said you were going to do it. Now I don't have to worry any more about when you're going to do it. And it does look much better,' she assured him.

His arms came around her in an exuberant hug. 'You are really starting to think like a sensible woman,' he breathed happily.

But it was the look in his eyes that tripped Jackie's heartbeat. She had only seen it once before in her life—when Geoff had asked her to marry him. And here it was again, compelling, binding, *loving*. Love, showering from his brilliant blue eyes in actinic rays. It staggered Jackie out of her mind, but she could not possibly doubt it.

Sunny King loved her. And it explained everything that had happened: why he was so good to her, so kind, so considerate. In one intense moment of humility Jackie vowed that she would never again do anything to hurt this man, even if she had to bite her tongue off.

'Come on down to my study,' he urged. 'There's someone I want you to meet and something I want you to see.'

He swept her along with him while Jackie was still mentally swept off her feet by the knowledge she had just acquired. A tall thin man with a long face was behind Sunny's desk and he nodded indulgently at her as Sunny performed introductions.

'Jackie, this is my architect, Jason Guthrie.'

Architect! Oh, no! No, no, no, her mind cried. 'Sunny, I don't want another house. If I want to build another house I'll do it myself. But I rather think I might buy somewhere else. I don't know yet what I'll do,' she pleaded anxiously.

He laughed and dropped a kiss on her forehead. 'It's not a house. Just a little pottery workshop. When I knocked your kiln down I certainly wasn't intending that you should do without one. Jason's drawn up some plans that I want you to look at very closely. They're very clever but they're still only preliminary sketches and you've got to tell him where he's gone wrong so he can get it exactly right. Precisely what you want and need.'

'That's right,' Jason Guthrie chimed in. 'We can do it any number of ways. The aim is to have it exactly right for you.'

She couldn't keep taking from Sunny King. It was parasitic. He saw the quandary of conscience in her eyes and immediately launched into persuasive appeal. 'Jackie, an artist of your creativity deserves the best. How can you do your works of genius if ...'

'But I ...' She couldn't accept it but she didn't want to hurt Sunny, either. Nor put him down in front of his architect. 'This is too much. I'm not a very good potter, Sunny. Really I'm not.'

He whipped around, picked some object off a shelf and held it out to her, his eyes sparkling with teasing humour. It nestled in the palm of his hand, and the awful recognition of her own handicraft sent Jackie into a paralytic shock. 'Anyone who can create something as magnificent as this can't be kept from her work,' Sunny declared triumphantly.

It was one of the llamas that Jackie had baked with such terrible animosity in her heart. Sunny King's face was immediately recognisable. Shame flooded through her. She peered up at him guiltily through half-lowered lashes. 'Sunny, I ... I'm so sorry, I ...'

'I'm not,' he chuckled. 'Best thing I've ever seen. One day it'll be a collector's piece. I'm buying all I can get my hands on. Give them to my friends as Christmas gifts. Now come and cast your eye over Jason's plans.'

Absolutely mortified by Sunny's pleasure in the llama, Jackie tamely acceded to his wishes. The workshop Jason Guthrie had sketched was any potter's dream. She nodded like an automaton as he explained the efficient grouping of the kilns and work benches, the shelf storage and every other thoughtful detail. Sunny beamed at her approval. He gave Jason Guthrie the go-ahead and the architect departed.

Jackie could not let the matter pass. She was consumed with guilt. As soon as they were alone she turned to Sunny in abject apology. 'It was wicked of me to put your face on those llamas.'

He grinned from ear to ear. 'They're certainly wicked.'

'Why aren't you mad at me?' she asked in bewilderment, then knew it was a stupid question. She knew the answer. He loved her.

His face softened as he drew her into a gently comforting embrace. 'Because when I found them, it was the first time I felt confident of success. That wickedly executed face meant I'd really got through to you. I have, haven't I?'

A self-conscious laugh gurgled up her throat. 'You're not wrong.' Then a flood of feeling that she did not stop to analyse made her reach up and wind her arms around his neck. 'Remember that first night when you wanted to show me your bedhead from Bali and I refused to look at it?'

'I remember it well,' he said. There was a deep note of longing in his voice.

'I'd like to see it now, Sunny,' she said softly.

The hands that had begun to gather her closer were suddenly still. His whole body held an unnatural stillness as his eyes searched hers. 'Not because of some mistaken sense of gratitude, Jackie,' he said as though forcing the words out, and the necessity for them hurt.

It was true that she wanted to give him what he desired, but not only because he had given her so much. There was no hesitation over her reply. 'It would never be for that reason, Sunny, I promise you. And I'm old enough to know my own mind.'

'Would you ever come to love me?'

The question carried a note of pleading and there was no easy answer this time. She reached up and kissed him. 'Believe me, I wouldn't want it . . . you . . . if I didn't feel . . . if I didn't want you, Sunny. I think there is a great chance of it working out right.'

A flicker of disappointment was instantly wiped out by warm optimism. 'It will be all right,' he declared. 'It has to be,' he muttered half under his breath as he turned her to walk with him.

It was strange, because she knew she wanted him, wanted to know him in the most intimate way of all, yet now that the moment of decision had come, Jackie felt increasingly nervous with each step they took towards his bedroom. She had never had sex with anyone apart from Geoff, and she probably wasn't very good at it anyway. Certainly not a match for a man of Sunny's experience. What if she failed to live up to his expectations? What if he was bored with her afterwards?

Sunny closed the bedroom door softly behind them. Apparently he was in no hurry, for he leaned back against the door, his hand gently holding hers.

She shot him a tense, apprehensive look and with a soft laugh he shook his head at her. 'You look like the kid who was caught stealing the apple.'

'More like Eve caught by Adam,' she retorted, giving vent to some of her pent-up emotion.

His smile offered her understanding. 'You have every right to be apprehensive, but I don't want you to be. Come here.' He gently tugged her hand and she took the step back to him. His arms slid around her. 'Hug me. Just be close to me,' he softly urged. 'I'll understand. I certainly won't have you doing anything you don't want to do.'

It was a relief to accept his embrace, to slide her arms around him and press into the warmth and strength of his body. It felt good, as if she belonged there. His hand ruffled through her hair, soothing, caressing, loving. There was no urging, no haste. He gave the impression of being content to stand there all day, for all the days of his life, just holding her.

She raised her head and his lips brushed lightly over hers, leaving and coming back in a slow, continual searching out of her response, ridding her of her inhibitions by never offering more than she wanted to receive, was eager to receive and give back.

She could never remember making love to Geoff except in the dark. It had been that kind of relationship, matter-of-fact rather than this deliberate incitement and enjoyment of sensuality. She did not think that Sunny would ever feel a need for darkness in order to give his love.

His fingers glided down her back, found nerve-endings that made her shiver with pleasure, yet still they felt incredibly soft, their contact not really firm, simply more intimate. His hand trailed slowly from her hair, across her neck, down her throat, stroking her skin softly to the top button of her blouse.

'It's all right, Jackie,' he whispered into her ear. 'I've seen how you look before . . . lovely, womanly, beautiful . . .'

Her mouth blindly sought his, wanting, needing its comfort, its reassurance, its excitement. And he answered her need with a sensitivity that completely drowned any possible apprehension.

The buttons were undone one by one, each a deliberate movement denying any thought of taking a sly advantage, almost a waiting for assurance of her consent. Then her blouse was opened, pushed gently from her arms, and it felt marvellous to press her naked breasts against him.

She wondered if she should be doing something, touching him, undoing his shirt, but when Sunny's hands came up to perform that operation himself, it seemed better to let their touch brush down the exquisite sensitivity of her bare flesh. It was even better when she was pressed against the warm smoothness of his naked chest.

He cradled her in his arms, rocking her gently as though she were a child, loving her with a tenderness that none the less held a soft, exciting yearning, a need to belong, to have and to hold, to possess. Jackie threw her arms around his neck to

cling even closer. Never had she felt such exciting
anticipation, such feverish desire.

His hands undid her skirt and pushed the
material down over her broad, firm hips, collecting
her briefs on the way; Jackie stepped out of them, a
slow deliberate step. She knew that she would not
have done this for any other man.

Sunny picked her up effortlessly and carried her
towards the bed, his lips playing a symphony of
longing and desire over her own. He opened the
curtaining on the four-poster with a sweep of one
hand and gently laid her down. He stood over her,
dominant, commanding, his eyes luminous with
passionate desire for her as he stripped off what was
left of his clothes. It was done without haste, with
an arrogant assurance that she would not change
her mind now.

The way his eyes lingered on her, examining her
in the minutest detail, was too much for Jackie,
filling her with a melting heat that almost made
her squirm. She stretched out her hand to him.
'Please ...' Her voice sounded furry, almost
unrecognisable.

He sat down next to her, his hands lightly
caressing erotic areas, awakening an exquisite
sensitivity to his touch. His head lowered over her,
his mouth tracing the path of his hands, and Jackie
gasped with each new contact, each delicate nuance
and sharp wave of pleasure. Her body was
exploding with vibrant sensations, nerve-endings
quivering with fierce delight, her arms and legs

aching from the melting weakness spreading
through them.

Sunny's body moved sensuously over her own.
She was going out of her mind with the need for a
resolution to the feelings he had aroused. Her
hands were running around the solidity of his
chest, scrabbling over the thickly muscled shoulders, raking down his back. He groaned. She
thought wildly that she should apologise, but he
moved his body to touch hers intimately, urgently,
and all thought fled from her mind as the muscles
in her thighs went entirely limp, quivering
helplessly as he gently spread her legs apart to
admit him.

When he entered her body she moved with him,
completely abandoning herself to the rhythm of his
making, wanting only to follow where he led,
wanting him to do with her as he pleased, pleasing
her with the pulsing strength of his desire.

His movements were slow and exquisite, a
delicate almost torturous preliminary to a passion
that gradually built to a wild pounding of satyric
pleasure. Jackie lost all control, her body a helpless
vessel that spasmed with ecstatic pleasure as he
plunged into her, his possession, and her total
surrender of self to his pleasure drove him wild. She
heard him crying out, felt the urgent, jerking
thrusts that strove for the ultimate climax, knew a
primitive exultation at the driving power of his
need, received him with a searing tenderness when
he finally collapsed on her, his breath coming in

hoarse gasps, his heart pounding its strained distress.

She sighed her contentment, at peace with the world and all that was in it. She glided her hands over his back, caressing and soothing, happy to give him the comfort he had given her. His arms hugged her tightly to him. His legs wound around hers, twining and intertwining as they moved languorously over the bed, shifting contacts, fingers and toes meeting, moving, melting together, savouring their togetherness. Never had after-sex felt so wonderfully close, so deliciously sensual, so gloriously right.

'Feel good?' Sunny murmured, nuzzling her ear to her squirming delight.

'Mmm.' She moved her foot up the calf of his leg. Fingers grazed teasingly over her sole and she laughed as she quickly stroked her foot down again. 'I'm not so sure about your bedhead, but you're a master craftsman, Sunny King.'

He gave a soft chuckle. 'I've never felt better in my life. We were made for each other, Jackie Mulholland.'

They lay there a long time, savouring their contentment. Then Sunny abruptly moved, shifting himself to rest on his side, his head propped up with one hand, eyes twinkling with sheer devilment as he gazed down at the placid satisfaction on her face.

'What are you thinking?' Jackie asked.

'I was wondering if it was possible to be any happier than I am now.'

'And what conclusion did you come to?'

Jackie squeaked at the provocative glide of his hand up her thigh. The look in his eyes grew alarmingly purposeful.

'I'm not going to die wondering about it,' he murmured into her ear.

And it didn't take very long at all to convince Jackie that she shouldn't die wondering about it either. What he was doing was absolutely right.

CHAPTER TEN

'CAN we go abseiling with Trevor, Mum?' Edmund blurted out over breakfast, earning a swift kick under the table from his elder brother.

Robert immediately put on his appeasing face. 'Not really abseiling, Mum. More like bush-walking, only we'll have ropes and things with us to make sure we're safe wherever we go and whatever happens.'

Jackie cut straight through the palaver. 'The answer is absolutely no. You are not going with Trevor under any circumstances, so you might as well forget it right now.' She fixed Trevor with a stern look of warning.

'Not my idea, Mrs Mulholland,' he said with a dismissive shrug. 'The boys asked me and I told them they had to ask you. In my hearing,' he added with an 'I told you so' look at the intrepid petitioners.

'Thank you, Trevor,' Jackie said with warm approval.

He was a trustworthy young man, she decided, which was probably why Sunny had hired him as his personal assistant. She was beginning to have a very healthy respect for Sunny's judgement of character. Betty Willis was a marvellously efficient and cheerful housekeeper, and her husband, Tom, was equally hard-working and always seemed to be available to lend a helping hand with anything.

Betty came in to clear the table and the boys stood up and helpfully gathered up their own used plates. 'We'll go for a ride on our bikes down the road,' Robert announced casually. 'If that's all right, Mum?'

'Yes,' she nodded, thankful that they hadn't decided to be argumentative. She had too big a problem on her mind to suffer being pestered by the boys. 'But be careful,' she added warningly. 'And take jumpers with you. It's cold today and it'll be even colder on a bike.' Although it was only the third week in May, the cold blustering winds outside announced that winter was definitely on its way.

'Could we take some fruit with us, Mrs Willis?' Edmund asked chirpily. 'In case we get hungry?'

'Of course you can,' Mrs Willis agreed, smiling indulgently at both boys. 'And there are cookies in the tin. I baked them specially for you yesterday.'

'Gee, thanks, Mrs Willis. You're a terrific cook,' Robert declared, pouring on the charm. 'Really great at cookies and cakes!'

Crawler, Jackie thought with a sudden appreciation of his potential with the ladies when he grew older. He had Betty Willis eating out of his hands already, and Edmund was learning fast. The kindly housekeeper would spoil them rotten if Jackie didn't keep a watchful eye on proceedings.

Though really, the boys hadn't given her any reason for complaint since they had burnt the house down. Their behaviour had been admirable, which had probably placed an almost intolerable strain on their systems. There was only one more day to go before the new school term began and so long as they didn't manage to kill themselves on their bikes before Monday she was hopeful of relative peace for some time to come. Her only immediate problem was her relationship with Sunny. She had to find out what was wrong.

A covert glance at him showed her he was wearing that distracted look again. She doubted that he had heard one word spoken over the table this morning. He was brooding over something and it was beginning to get to her. His mood had been very much less than sunny for the last couple of days.

Was he bored with her now that she had given in to him? It worried Jackie. Didn't he want her here any more? Suddenly he stood up, excused himself from the table and headed off without one personal word to her. Jackie realised she found it more than worrying.

She looked over at Trevor, needing some hint of what was wrong, because something definitely was. If Sunny was disappointed in their relationship she couldn't hang on here, no matter how reluctant she felt to leave him. 'Do you know what's worrying Sunny, Trevor?'

'I ... er ... don't think it's for me to say, Mrs Mulholland. You'll have to ask Sunny,' he finished in a mumble, his eyes evading her direct gaze. He immediately pushed himself to his feet and excused himself to go and catch up on some overdue paperwork.

Jackie was left alone and she felt utterly miserable, shut off and unwanted. She trailed off to the laundry to do some washing. There was nothing else for her to do around the house since Mrs Willis reigned in the kitchen and two cleaning ladies came in every day to keep the place spick and span.

Her mind fretted over the problem with Sunny. Something was definitely wrong and she felt deeply hurt that he chose not to discuss it with her. She wanted to share more than her bed with him. Their relationship was too one-sided. Sunny gave her everything he possibly could, and she was unable to reciprocate except with the pleasure she gave him when they made love.

Somehow that seemed insignificant now. Since he wasn't communicating with her in any other way, he obviously thought she couldn't supply whatever it was he needed. It made her feel totally inadequate. And the possibility that she might be losing him made her feel even worse. She decided she would have to get to the root of the problem but was undecided on how best to go about it.

She filled in the morning trying out sketches for future creations in clay, but her mind wasn't on the task. Sunny didn't even appear for lunch and Mrs Willis informed her that he had been down in the theatre all morning and had told her he didn't want to be disturbed. Disappointment acted as a spur and Jackie decided she had to take the bull by the horns. She made up a plateful of sandwiches and took it down to the theatre.

She gave a courtesy knock on the door, then opened it quickly before Sunny had a chance to tell her to go away. She caught the familiar face of Dirk Vescum on the screen before she spotted Sunny hunched over on the far sofa, his head in his hands, not even watching the movie, obviously not aware of her entrance either. She walked over to him, the thick carpet muffling her footsteps. She had to touch him to draw his attention.

Sunny's head jerked up. On the instant of recognition his hand flashed to the table for the remote control. The screen blanked out and the overhead light blinked on. 'Jackie?' The vaguely quizzical note in his voice told her she had interrupted a deep concentration and it was clearly a struggle for him to bring his mind to bear on her unexpected appearance.

A sense of guilt frayed her confidence but the damage was done now. She was here with him and she had to speak up. 'I thought you might like some lunch. And I wanted to talk to you.' She set the plate of sandwiches on the table in front of him and tried an encouraging smile.

'Something wrong?' he asked, making Jackie realise that she usually only sought him out to voice some frustration or other. She suddenly felt ashamed of how self-centred she had been.

'What's wrong with us, Sunny? What's wrong with me?' she blurted out without any preamble.

He looked astonished. 'How can you think such a

thing? There's nothing wrong with you. You're perfect,' he insisted staunchly.

'But you're not happy.'

'I am. I couldn't be more so.'

'No, you're not. You've been brooding over something for days. Please tell me the truth.'

Her obvious distress caused him to pause and frown. Still frowning he shot her a guarded look. 'It's the movie. It's not right and I don't know how to fix it.' The admission was reluctant and clearly painful to him.

'Tell me about it,' she asked quietly.

He shook his head. 'I'll work it out eventually.'

With a flash of insight, Jackie remembered how unfair she had been in her criticism of his movies before she had seen them. If Sunny didn't think the movie was right, then he would be wary of her opinion. She had hurt him in her blind prejudice and might hurt him again. Where she was concerned he was particularly vulnerable. He wanted her approval, her admiration. It would be going against his grain to admit anything that he would consider a failure on his part.

'Please, Sunny, won't you let me share this with you?' she begged, and was surprised at the urgent need in her voice.

It surprised him, too. His eyes focused sharply on her, questioning. 'I don't want to bore you, Jackie. You can't really care about . . .'

'I care about you,' she interrupted softly, and it was true. She really did care about what he thought and felt.

A warm, happy glow lit Sunny's eyes and he took her hand and drew her down on to his lap. He smiled as she uninhibitedly threw her arms around his neck and snuggled closer. Then he kissed her and his hand closed softly over one breast.

Jackie sucked in a deep, determined breath and pulled his hand away. 'Not now, Sunny,' she told him firmly.

'No?' His eyebrows arched in provocative disbelief.

'I can't think when you do that, and I need to share everything with you. Lovemaking isn't enough. It never would be.'

'But there's nothing I like better than making love to you,' he argued, placing persuasive little kisses around her face.

'Please, don't cut me off.'

He sighed and surrendered. 'You're right.' He fell into brooding again for a long time before he continued. 'The truth is I'm satisfied with the movie. That's not the problem. It's the music. It's just not doing what I want it to do and I can't figure out what it needs. All I know is that it's wrong.'

The confession really pained him. Jackie could feel the hurt emanating from him with every word he had forced out. She wondered if this was the first time he had ever confessed to failure. If so, it was a very big thing he had done for her.

'Show me the movie, Sunny,' she urged softly. 'Let me hear how it sounds. I'd like to see what you've done, anyway. Then we can talk about it.'

He hesitated, obviously not liking her to see the

imperfect product, then he took in the sincere appeal in her eyes and shrugged. 'If that's what you want.'

He sat her on the sofa and reset the tape of the movie back to its beginning. Jackie kicked off her sandals and settled herself comfortably next to him, preparing for a long session of full concentration. She was not about to criticise his failing at something. What really mattered was being allowed to share his failures as well as his successes. Sunny threw her a half-wary, vulnerable look; then, with a resigned sigh, he pressed the appropriate buttons on his remote control panel.

The movie was entitled *Strike At The Heart* and from the very opening scene Jackie was enthralled with it. The story revolved around the plan for the ultimate destruction of the aliens' headquarters. Dirk Vescum showed his love for Alena by becoming more and more protective of her. At one particularly desperate part of the action, Dirk's forces were being annihilated when Alena arrived to join him. His despair at seeing her was written over his face as he fiercely rejected her support, and her love for him was equally moving as she fiercely counter-challenged him with the steely words, 'Do you think I would want to live without you?'

The fighting action that followed was hectic edge-of-the-seat stuff that had Jackie's heart in her mouth all the way until the final resolution. She was barely aware of the music until the climax of the battle. The aliens' headquarters was being bombarded—explosions, fire, chaos everywhere—

and then she knew exactly what Sunny meant. The action was spectacular. It cried out for a spectacular burst of music to highlight it and generate the feeling of awesome triumph. Something tremendously climactic. And what was there was wrong.

'Play that last part again, Sunny,' she asked as the movie ended. She was almost sure she knew what was needed.

Sunny groaned in despair. 'It's hopeless, isn't it? I'll have to get another composer. Another score. But how to tell them what I want when I don't know myself? That's the hell of it.'

Impelled by his pained outburst to offer solace, Jackie didn't hesitate any longer. 'Sunny, the music you need ... I think it might already have been written.' She jumped to her feet in excitement. 'Wait here! I'll be right back. I think I've got what you want,' she babbled and was off before he could say a word.

She raced up the stairs to her room and tore open the box of compact discs that Sunny had bought her. She had stubbornly refused to play them and he had stubbornly refused to send them back. She sorted through them in purposeful haste and triumphantly pounced on the recordings she was looking for, Wagner's *Götterdämmerung*—Twilight of the Gods—the final opera of the *Ring* quartet, and *The Ride of the Valkyries*. If Sunny couldn't see how this music fitted his concept then he was a ... a troglodyte. She skipped back down the stairs to the theatre.

'Can we play the compact discs in here?' she cried excitedly.

'What have you got?' Sunny asked, eyes suspicious at her enthusiasm.

'The music, of course! You'll have to be patient with me while I find the exact places on the discs. Then I'll play the music for you while you play the climax of the movie without any other sound. Then you'll see.'

He shook his head, somewhat bemused, but he helped her to the necessary equipment and waited, watching her with quizzical eyes until she found what she wanted. At her direction he rewound the film to the critical point where the music had failed to grab the essence of the action.

'Now watch and listen,' she commanded, hoping he would see what she was trying to show him.

In unison they pressed the necessary controls. The mighty music of Wagner swelled into the room in crashing waves, building with huge dramatic force towards its magnificent, thunderous climax, evoking the awesome image of Valhalla in flames, of Valhalla falling, of Valhalla being destroyed.

After that she instantly switched to *The Ride of the Valkyries*, with its soaring chords of triumph. To Jackie these pieces of music were amongst the most soul-stirring ever composed and she was certain that their sheer grandeur would have to appeal to Sunny. She was right. He sat through it absolutely mesmerised, watching his film, hearing the music.

Only when the last note echoed into silence did he bounce up, rubbing his hands together in exultant glee. 'Do that to me again!' he commanded.

She played the music over and over. They tried to synchronise the action to the music a little better and Sunny was sparkling with elation at the effect produced. He grabbed Jackie and whirled her around.

'I've got it! I've got it! I knew I could do it, you marvellous woman!' he cried, giving her an exuberant hug before putting her down so he could pace around in a fever of excitement. 'I can see it now. That's the material to use. We'll jazz it up. Make it really big. Use three orchestras. Intersperse it with a rock band. I know exactly how to do it now.'

A rock band! Intersperse Wagner's great music with a rock band! All Jackie's delight at providing the answer to Sunny's problem was instantly crushed by a mountain of horror, quickly followed by a tidal wave of furious indignation. Her mouth opened. Her brain tossed around venomous words. Her voice lifted to shrilling pitch.

'You phil . . .'

Sunny turned to her, his face still alight with happy triumph. Her mouth bit down on her tongue, cutting off the word, philistine, in mid-shrill. Her brain abruptly changed gears and whirled again. Hadn't she wanted to make him happy? And what right did she have to be so arrogant in her judgements?

You need a bit of humility, Jackie Mulholland, she warned herself. You're not always right. Sunny King had proved time and time again that he knew what he was doing when he was making movies for the market. Horses for courses, she reminded herself fiercely.

Sunny frowned at her tightly clamped mouth. 'What did you say I was?' he asked warily.

Jackie put on a belated smile. 'A philomel,' she replied with lilting innocence. Sometimes it was really useful to have a good vocabulary.

Sunny's responding smile held an uncertain tilt. 'What does that mean?'

She waltzed up to him and hung her arms around his neck, her eyes softly teasing him. 'Oh, somebody who makes music like a nightingale. Like you.'

The elation came back in a delighted grin. 'Jackie, you're the most wonderful woman in the whole world. I knew my instincts were right when I first saw you, sleeping in the moonlight on the veranda. I knew then you had to be mine. And I was right.'

For some reason the blatant arrogance of that speech didn't matter because the love in his eyes more than made up for it, and when he kissed her she was very, very glad that she had held her tongue, because the sweet hunger of his kiss was far more satisfying than any amount of intellectual pride.

'Mum! Mum!'

The urgent cries broke them apart as Edmund

burst into the room, his small face white and terrified.

'Robert's caught below a ledge. I couldn't pull him up. The ropes have knotted on the overhang. I tried and tried,' he panted out in hopeless distress.

'My God! You went abseiling!' Jackie cried, her heart cramping with fear even as she made the accusation.

'Where is he, Edmund?' Sunny snapped out.

'Up the mountain at the end of the road. Where Trevor took us the last time,' Edmund replied.

'I told you not . . .' Jackie began, despair adding its bite to her heart.

'We didn't! You told us not to go with Trevor, so we went by ourselves. Robert figured . . .'

'No time for that,' Sunny whipped in. 'It's cold outside and it'll be dark soon. We've got to move.'

And he was off, yelling out for Trevor, roaring orders. 'Alert the Police Rescue Squad. Get an ambulance. And the Westpac Rescue Helicopter. Anybody else who can help. Betty, bring blankets to the Range Rover. And Tom, you bring ropes and torches. The big spotlights.'

Before she had time to think Jackie was pushed into the Range Rover. Sunny King slammed the four-wheel drive vehicle into gear and pressed the accelerator flat to the floor. For once, Jackie had no criticism of his propensity for speed.

She looked anxiously at the sky. The afternoon had slipped away while she and Sunny had been down in the theatre. At most there would only be an hour left before darkness fell. A bitterly cold wind had blown up. Robert had already been under that unprotected ledge, hanging suspended in mid-air, for over two and a half hours.

She turned to Edmund who was huddled on the back seat of the Range Rover. 'Has Robert got his jumper on?'

Edmund shook his head miserably. 'We took them off and left them on the top of the cliff before he went down. I tried to throw it to him, Mum, but I threw it too far out and he couldn't catch it. And the same thing happened with my own.'

The clutch of fear deepened. If they couldn't haul Robert up, if he had to stay there overnight . . . Geoff had died like that, hanging in mid-air, frozen to death before anyone could help.

A warm hand clasped her knee. She darted a distracted look at Sunny. 'We'll make it there before dark. We'll get him up. No point in thinking negative thoughts, Jackie,' he said quietly.

'No,' she agreed shakily, and breathed a silent prayer of thanks that Sunny was with her. No one else had ever given her such strong unfailing support. And she needed every bit of it to get through what lay ahead of them.

CHAPTER ELEVEN

SUNNY drove at a hectic pace, with total disregard for tyres, condition of the road, any impediment whatsoever, and the Range Rover was up on top of the cliff face in less than fifteen minutes. Jackie endured Sunny's mad recklessness without a word, grateful for it in this race against time. It had started to rain, cold lashing sheets of it, and the thought of Robert being wet as well as cold was enough to chill her to the bone.

'Over there!' Edmund shouted, pointing to the ropes as they jumped out of the vehicle.

The wind was bitingly cold, the rain pouring down in drenching ferocity. Sunny didn't hesitate. He ran for the cliff edge. Jackie followed on his heels. Suddenly sensing her presence behind him, he turned and threw her back.

'Are you mad, woman?' he roared at her. 'Don't come any closer, it's too dangerous. This wind is enough to blow you off and I won't be responsible for your death. Now get back to safety at once. And keep Edmund away, too.'

Edmund . . . of course. God! She wasn't thinking sensibly at all. He was panting on her heels, not to be left out of any rescue attempt. She turned, snatched up his hand and hauled him back to a safe distance. They watched Sunny crawl to the cliff edge, heard him hollering downwards. The words were whipped away with the wind. He crawled back a few yards, then sprang to his feet and ran to the Range Rover. He opened up the back and dragged out a rope before Jackie could even reach him.

'What's happening?' she cried, plucking desperately at his arm. 'Is ... is Robert all right?'

He clutched her shoulder in a steadying manner, his eyes commanding her not to panic. 'He's a long way down. Over a hundred feet. I thought I heard him answer.'

She swallowed hard. 'What ... what are we going to do?' Already the sky was darkening ominously, the clouds obliterating the light.

'You and Edmund are to stand here. Shine the big spotlight torches so that the helicopter can see where we are when it comes. And anyone else who might be along to help.'

Then he was striding away from her, stopping at a sturdy iron-bark, tying the end of the rope around the tree. She ran after him, unable to control the panic that was clawing at her heart.

'What are you going to do?' The words came out on a near-hysterical sob, and the sobs kept shaking out of her.

Sunny threw her a hard glare. 'I'm going down to untangle the bloody ropes while there's still some light left. For God's sake, get a hold on yourself!'

She tried but the sobs couldn't be stopped. 'Can't ... can't we just ... pull Robert up?'

'Do you want him battered to death against the overhang?' he demanded fiercely.

'No ... no-o ...'

'Then we'll do it my way.' He began to tie the rope around his chest, under his shoulders.

Jackie reached out a trembling hand to touch him. 'Sunny ...' She managed to swallow down a sob, her eyes imploring his patience. 'Sunny, do you know what you're doing?'

He smiled his love at her. 'Of course I do.'

She sighed in grateful relief.

A boyish grin lit his face. 'I had a lot of practice at it when I was in Holland.'

He was off before she could say another word, paying out the rope, edging back towards the cliff. Then into her churning mind came the nerve-shattering realisation. As far as Jackie knew, there wasn't even a hill in Holland, let alone a real mountain.

In glazed shock she watched Sunny drop the rope over the edge, saw it tighten in his hand as he reached the cliff face, saw the grimly determined set of his facial muscles as he eased himself over the ledge. Then he was gone, into the gathering gloom, the howling wind and the sheets of rain.

Another realisation hit her with even more shocking force. Sunny wasn't abseiling, he didn't have two ropes, only the one. And he was going down that rope hand over hand. Over a hundred feet to the overhang, he had said. And then he would be holding on to his rope with one hand while he tried to unravel Robert's tangled ropes with the other. It was impossible. It couldn't be done. Sunny was bound to fall. And when he did the knotted rope around his chest would either break every rib in his body or squeeze him to death.

Jackie wrung her hands in grieving despair, forced to acknowledge her impotence to help. How could she have let Sunny go? He was bound to to be killed, even more certainly than Robert. Geoff had taught her enough about abseiling to know that Robert's only risk came from the elements. Sunny King was risking his life. For her son. And for her.

A hand tucked around her arm. 'Don't cry, Mum. It'll be all right now. Robert's strong. He can take anything. He won't be hurt,'

She looked down into Edmund's fear-filled eyes, so bravely trying to be brave, and she took him in her arms, hugging him with a fierce mother-love. 'I know that, darling. We'll get Robert back.' Please, God, she prayed, let them both be safe.

It grew darker, the rain a relentless downpour, the wind a howling dervish, gusting up the valley in whirling bursts. The conditions made any chance of survival a torturous nightmare. Jackie watched the rope, willing the thread of life to remain steady. If the rope went slack then Sunny would have fallen. She kept her fingers on it, feeling the tension and every slight movement. She found herself mumbling a litany. 'Please, God, keep it tight. Don't let him fall.'

Edmund tugged at her coat. 'Mum, we should have the torches on.'

'Of course. You're right, Edmund.'

'And we should put the headlights of the Range Rover on, Mum. They'll be a lot more powerful than the torches.'

Why hadn't she thought of that herself? She had to control her emotions, think clearly. Lives depended on it. 'Thank you Edmund. Yes. We should do that straight away.'

But it was hard to leave the rope. She had to force herself to follow the lead of her son. No sooner had she switched the headlights on than she heard the noise, the heavy beat of the rotor-blades from a far distance. It cleared her mind to razor-sharpness.

'Edmund, take the torches and place them at right angles in the clearing over there, so that the beams of light intersect at the middle of it.'

The very act of decision helped her to pull herself together. She had to keep control, do the right things, act in the way that would best help Sunny and Robert. She heard the helicopter drawing rapidly closer, going out over the cliff edge. A huge spotlight flashed on, illuminating what was happening below. She checked to see that Edmund had the torches aligned correctly. The helicopter hovered overhead, then slowly, ever so slowly, started to descend.

At last help was at hand. Relief flooded through Jackie. Hang on, Sunny, hang on, Robert, she silently chanted. We'll have you up in no time. She turned on a buoyant step and looked at the rope attached to the iron-bark, clearly outlined in the glow from the Range Rover's headlights.

It had gone completely slack!

Pain stabbed her heart. She sank to her knees, a cry of distress screaming straight from her soul. She closed her eyes, hugged her arms tightly around the piercing ache and keened for Sunny King, for the life of a man she had come to love, a man so opposite to her yet so inexpressibly dear, so . . .

'Cease that boo-hooing at once, Jackie. Is that any way to greet a man back? And there's still a bit of work to be done yet.'

For one stunned, disbelieving moment, Jackie stared uncomprehendingly at the face above her: Sunny's face, pale from fatigue, water dripping down it, but Sunny's face nevertheless.

'I've done it,' he told her proudly. 'The ropes are untangled; we can haul him up. And I've spoken to Robert. Nothing wrong with him.'

Jackie flew at him, hurling her arms around him, heart pounding a paean of joy and relief. 'Thank God you're safe! You're both safe!'

'Dirk Vescum looks after his own.' Sunny declared with grand smugness.

Jackie began to giggle. Hysterically. He was a child, nothing but a big, grown-up child. Or was he simply being facetious to relax her tension? She swallowed the mad giggle and raised hesitant eyes, probing the darkness of his eyes, trying to probe into the heart of him.

'What's going on here?' It was the bark of authority.

Sunny tucked Jackie under his arm and faced two burly men. 'Abseil the boy up. I'm pretty well beat,' he said on a telling sigh.

'No trouble,' one of the men said cheerfully.

'Hey, Mum! I came up under my own steam,' a chirpy voice informed her.

'Robert!' Jackie whirled out of Sunny's arms and gathered her wilful, wayward son into a crushing embrace.

'Hey! Go easy, Mum,' he protested.

'Are you hurt?' she asked anxiously, instantly loosening her hold.

'Nah! It was a breeze.'

'A breeze!' Jackie choked.

'Isn't there anything for us to do?' came the critical voice of authority. It sounded disappointed.

'Bit of a false alarm,' Sunny declared off-handedly.

'Well, we still have to take the boy to hospital.'

Jackie swung around to face the spokesman, her heart leaping in agitation at the idea of Robert having to go to hospital.

A genial face smiled at her and a beefy hand was thrust out. 'I'm Dr Meares. Mrs Mulholland, is it? Mother of the boy?'

She weakly grasped his hand and nodded.

'It's just for observation. One night in hospital won't hurt him. No need for alarm. Rules and regulations, you know. He looks perfectly all right to me but we must follow form.'

'But . . .'

'Now don't worry, dear.' The doctor patted her hand. 'There's no need for you to come. We'll just

take the boy along with us and pop him in for the
night.'

'But is it necessary?' Jackie demanded anxiously.

The doctor shook his head. 'Not necessary. Not
necessary at all. But we've got to do it. Rules and
regulations in these rescue cases.' His face suddenly
broke into a ribald grin. 'We had one case where we
were called in. Woman had apparently died while
having sex—only passed out really. By the time we
got there she had quite recovered. Had to pull the
husband off her. But we got her to hospital for
observation. Rules and regulations. Can't go
against them.'

'You've never passed out on me,' Sunny growled
in Jackie's ear.

She ignored him, although a silly smile was
tugging at her mouth. 'But, Doctor . . .' she said
firmly.

'Aw, Mum! Don't spoil it,' Robert pleaded. 'I've
never been in a helicopter.'

'Robert, don't you interrupt your mother,'
Sunny said sternly. 'You've done quite enough
interrupting for one afternoon.'

'Yessir,' Robert mumbled humbly.

'It's only for twenty-four hours, Mrs Mulholland,' the doctor explained. 'You can come and
collect him tomorrow. If you want to,' he added
with an arch look at Robert.

Jackie gave in. The doctor took hold of Robert
and marched him over to the helicopter. Edmund
mumbled something about Robert always having
all the luck, which earned a sharp reprimand from

Sunny and a short lecture on the worry they had
both given their mother. They stood in the rain and
watched the safe departure of rules and regulations.

Sunny's arm curled around Jackie's shoulders,
holding her with him as he spoke sternly to her
younger son. 'Edmund, into the car!'

'Yessir,' he answered meekly, and scooted.

'Now, Jackie . . .'

His hand slid away. He walked about in
considerable agitation, smacking his hands together as if beating up determined purpose. The
rain was pouring down on both of them, but Jackie
didn't think of suggesting that they should also
return to the car. Her attention was entirely
focused on this extraordinary man that she loved.

He shook an emphatic finger at her. 'Those boys
of yours need discipline.' Spoken in the manner of a
proclamation.

'Yes, I can see that,' she said demurely.

'Things cannot be permitted to go on the way
they've been going.'

'You're right.'

'Those boys need a father. They desperately
need a father.'

'It would be good for them.'

He stepped up and measured her, eyeball to
eyeball. 'If they don't get a father soon, they'll be
dead. And so will you. They need someone they
admire and respect to take control, to . . .' He
floundered for words.

'To rule them with a rod of iron,' Jackie supplied
helpfully, her heart soaring with love for him.

Surprise flickered over his face. 'You agree with me?'

'Absolutely.'

'I can do it, Jackie. I'd be good for them. Once I was at the helm, they wouldn't step out of line. They need someone like me. Control and discipline. It's for your own good, Jackie. And theirs.' He was almost pleading.

She smiled all her love at him. 'Sunny, there is no one in the whole world like you.'

He frowned suspiciously at her. 'Do you really mean that?'

She remembered all she had thought and felt while he had been down on the cliff face. 'I know it,' she said fervently.

His eyes searched hers anxiously. 'I wouldn't let you go, you know. Lifetime job. Total commitment. Nothing less would satisfy.

She looked up at him dreamily. 'You are a beautiful, beautiful man, Sunny King.'

'Living with me all the time ... you might not like that,' he continued, almost as if he hadn't heard her, or couldn't quite believe her. 'I know I'm not perfect. Though I wouldn't say that to anyone else. But you'd have to be happy with me, Jackie. Your needs, your wants, are more important to me than my own.'

'I'd do anything for you, Sunny. Anything at all.'

'When will you marry me?' he instantly demanded.

'As soon as you like,' she sighed blissfully.

He wrapped her in an iron-tight embrace and poured kisses all over her head. 'You're getting wet, Jackie,' he sighed. 'I think it's raining. We'd better go home.'

'Yes. Home,' she agreed even more blissfully.

He bundled her into the Range Rover, wrapped a blanket around her, then took the driver's seat. In a totally uncharacteristic move, he drove home at a sedate, safety-conscious pace, a smile never leaving his lips and one hand firmly enfolding one of Jackie's.

It seemed that all the lights in the house were on. The garage door was open. Betty and Tom Willis were standing there with Trevor, waiting to do anything that was required. Their welcoming smiles said they already knew that Robert had been safely rescued. As soon as the Range Rover pulled to a halt, Trevor had the back door open and Edmund hoisted into his arms.

'You little monkey,' he said affectionately. 'Don't you ever do that without me again.'

'Get him into a bath, Trevor,' Sunny ordered as he swiftly alighted. 'Betty, look after him, will you? Feed him and put him to bed?'

'Of course I will,' the housekeeper agreed, already fussing over Edmund.

Jackie was still trying to untangle herself from the blanket when Sunny opened her door and swept her up into his arms. 'I'm all right. I can walk,' she protested feebly.

'I'm going to put you in the sauna. Stop you getting a cold. Most important,' Sunny muttered, cradling her even closer to him.

'Need my help, Sunny?' Tom Willis asked.

'No thanks, Tom. This case needs my care. My particular loving care,' he murmured, brushing his warm mouth across Jackie's forehead.

She had no inclination whatsoever to protest against that. As far as she was concerned, Sunny was the boss. And always would be. She could not be in better hands, hands that she knew would protect her, support her, love her; and what more could she possibly want? He was a man amongst men, Sunny King. The very best.

CHAPTER TWELVE

EDMUND begged to accompany them on the drive to pick up Robert from Royal Prince Alfred Hospital in Sydney. He had never been inside a big hospital and he didn't see why Robert should always have all the advantages. Although, of course, he was also concerned about seeing for himself that Robert was all right.

Sunny laughingly agreed that Edmund should come with them. His good humour was so expansive this morning that Jackie privately thought he would agree to anything. However, she herself was somewhat troubled. While she had no doubts about her feelings for Sunny—the acute sense of loss she had experienced last night left no room for doubt at all on that issue—her commitment to him did pose some practical problems.

For one thing, she couldn't be sure how the boys would react to the news. While they admired and liked Sunny, she also knew they revered the memory of their father. She decided that she would sound them out gradually on the idea of remarriage.

The other factor that worried her was the lack of common interests between herself and Sunny. From her experience of being married to Geoff, Jackie knew how important it was for a married couple to be able to share and talk about things

together. Without those common bonds to link
them it was all too easy for people to drift apart, no
matter how much they loved one another.

She pondered on these problems while Sunny
drove them into the city in the Diamler. To
Edmund's disgust and Jackie's relief, the whole
trip was negotiated at a very conservative speed.
When they arrived at the hospital they found
Robert chatting up the patients and staff. As Dr
Meares had assured Jackie the night before, her
irresponsible son had suffered no harm at all from
his perilous escapade, but she said quite a few
wounding words to him on the way home to make
up for it.

A couple of days slipped by and Jackie threw out
several leading comments to the boys, but she
hadn't actually declared her intention to marry
Sunny when he himself raised the issue and a few
other matters. It was late at night and they were
lying on their bed in the warm afterglow of
satisfaction given and received.

'Have you spoken to the boys yet?' he suddenly
asked.

Jackie sighed, feeling a little bit guilty about her
hesitancy. She didn't want Sunny to feel slighted in
any way. 'I've been hinting at it but I haven't
actually told them yet. I think I'll do it tomorrow,'
she said cautiously.

She might just as well have saved herself the bit
of heartburn. 'There won't be any trouble there,'
he said with his usual arrogant confidence.

A niggle of exasperation crept into her voice.
'How can you be so sure?'

'They think I'm wonderful,' he said modestly.

A giggle tickled her throat but she swallowed it down with a smile. 'So do I, but I'm not certain that will be enough for them.'

'You'll see,' Sunny said confidently. 'However, there is one problem we do have to resolve.'

'What's that?' Jackie asked, feeling alarmed that Sunny also saw a problem for them.

'This house.'

'What's wrong with it?'

'You don't like it.'

'I do, I do, I do,' Jackie sang in sheer relief that the problem was not a problem at all.

'You said you didn't. You said ...'

'I've changed my mind,' she insisted.

He looked at her suspiciously. 'For a clever woman, you change your mind a lot.'

'That's because of you.'

'What do I do?'

She grinned her love at him. 'You strike at the heart. And that changes any woman's perception of things.'

For a moment he grinned back in pleasure, but a frown quickly gathered again. 'Are you sure? If you want to redecorate ...'

'The only thing I'd change ...' Jackie commenced firmly.

'Yes?'

'... are those rotten statues.'

'I'll get Tom Willis to take them to the dump tomorrow. What will you put in their place?'

'Wait and see.' She smiled her contentment. Somehow Sunny's compulsive need to see to her happiness put her mind at rest. Her eyes caressed him with a deep gratitude that he was her man. 'Why have you never married, Sunny?' she asked, thinking how terribly lucky she was that he hadn't.

He thought for a minute, then replied, 'There were two reasons. Most of my life I lived in abject poverty and I'd never subject a woman I loved to that.'

'And the second?'

He rolled on to his side and looked down at her, smiling as he stroked her cheek with featherlight tenderness. 'I'd never met anyone I truly admired until I met you. Certainly no one I ever loved.'

And Jackie's contentment stretched to an even deeper level. In fact, she felt so good that, when morning came, it didn't take too much courage at all to broach the boys with the announcement that she and Sunny were getting married. However, their reaction immediately dimmed her happiness.

'No, Mum! You're not!' Robert said in shocked tones. 'You can't!'

'We don't believe it!' Edmund joined in with even more shock. 'Don't do it, Mum!'

Tears welled into Jackie's eyes.

'Aw, gee, Mum! Don't get upset,' Robert begged in an instant *volte-face*. 'We were only joking. Truly we were. We knew you were going to marry Sunny, and we thought it would be fun to pull your leg a bit.'

'Yeah. We knew ever since we saw you kissing Sunny in his bedroom that night we came up to watch the party,' Edmund informed her smugly.

Robert looked equally smug as he added, 'It was

obvious that it was only a matter of time, Mum, so
we decided ...'

'You don't really mind?' Jackie asked dazedly.

They answered in enthusiastic tandem, 'No, we
think it's great ...'

'Having a Dad at long last ...'

'Should have done it years ago, Mum ...'

'Months ago, anyway. When Sunny first asked
you ...'

'We wouldn't have had to do all that painting ...'

'Yeah. Best thing we ever did was burn down the
house ...'

'Though we didn't mean it at the time,
Mum ...'

Jackie just shook her head and wandered away,
too relieved to bother taking them to task about
anything. Besides, Sunny had said he would do that
from now on, and, God knew, he would learn soon
enough how big a responsibility he had shouldered.

Having received her sons' blessing, Jackie confidently went ahead with the wedding arrangements.
Sunny was no help. When she asked him where he
wanted to go for their honeymoon, his eyes went all
dreamy and he replied, 'It doesn't matter. Wherever you like. I'd be happy anywhere with you.'

Jackie decided that Surfers' Paradise on the
Queensland Gold Coast was probably the best
place. It was only a thousand kilometres away and it
wouldn't be too dreadfully expensive. She was
finalising the arrangements when Sunny wandered
into the room that had been allotted as her study, a
look of absolute bliss on his face.

'I've found it, Jackie, and I've done it!'

A now-familiar tingle of apprehension crept down her spine. 'What have you found and what have you done?' she asked warily.

'I've chartered a sailing boat. Big. Really big. A hundred and twenty feet long. Fully crewed. We'll cruise around the Pacific islands then down the South American coast for our honeymoon. We'll be waited on hand and foot. Not a stroke of work has to be done. Just stay with each other and enjoy the balmy days and nights . . .'

Jackie looked at the booking arrangements on her desk, carefully screwed up the forms and dropped them in the wastepaper basket. She stood up and slipped into his enthusiastic embrace. 'I couldn't think of anything more perfect,' she agreed.

He beamed down at her. 'You're the most sensible woman I've ever met.'

Someone had to be sensible in this crazy house, she thought ruefully, but when the madness was divine, it was much easier to be swept along with it. Although she found herself shaking her head a lot, like over the issue of her dieting. Jackie thought she would look better if she lost a few pounds but Sunny instantly put a halt to that.

'You're not to deprive me of any bit of you,' he declared.

Which was fine by her. If Sunny liked her exactly as she was, so much the better. And really she didn't look too bad. But then he went on to declare, 'Jackie, for the rest of your life, you're only to do what you want to do.'

That was a bit much, coming on top of his order to stop dieting, but she suppressed a tart comment because she knew he was speaking from the heart.

Jackie made a major discovery in the weeks that led up to their wedding. It wasn't sharing things that made a relationship work. It was giving your partner what they needed. Sunny was such a compulsive giver to her that Jackie was in no doubt about his love, and she found that the more she adopted his approach and gave to him, the greater her love for him became.

By the time their wedding day arrived, she had come to the realisation that there was nothing she would not do to make him happy and contented. Sunny had taught her so much about loving that she felt very humble indeed, recognising at last just how much she had missed out on life.

They were married in the little historic church at St Alban's, thus presenting respectability in its most traditional form to all the local inhabitants, and erasing any possible blot on Jackie's reputation. The popular opinion was that it was a good thing, since Jackie Mulholland was a straight, level-headed woman who deserved a decent kind of man.

The honeymoon was all Sunny had promised it would be and they came home on a blissful wave of contentment. Trevor met them in the Daimler and transported them back to St Alban's. Robert and Edmund were at the front door to greet them, their faces lit with joyous welcome.

'It's grand to have you back, Mum,' Robert piped at her. 'And you, too, Dad.'

'Yeah. Dad. We love you, too,' Edmund added in

a burst of feeling.

Jackie beamed at them proudly. They hadn't had
any prompting. Their acceptance of Sunny as their
dad, their loving welcome ... they were behaving
just as she had always wished they would behave.
Her heart swelled with happiness. Sunny had said
they needed a father and the improvement in their
conduct was evident already.

Sunny clapped them on the shoulder. 'Good to
be back, boys.'

'Ah, Dad ...'

'Yes, Robert?'

'While Trevor was ... er ... picking you and
Mum up ...'

'Yes?'

'I was teaching Edmund how to drive ... the
Lagonda ...'

'And this tree ran into the road,' Edmund put in
appealingly.

'And crashed straight into the radiator,' Robert
finished quickly.

Jackie felt herself go faint.

A bull-like roar issued from her new husband.
'That's it!' He glowered with rage. 'That's the end!
Solitary confinement! Neither of you are to see a
movie, watch television, go anywhere, do anything, for a whole week. And if you disobey me I'll
whip your bottoms so hard you'll never walk
again.' His voice rose several decibels. 'Nor drive a
car!'

He swept a commanding arm towards the
staircase. 'Go! You are banished to your rooms.
The death penalty for disobedience. I don't want to

see your faces again for seven days. Except for coming and going to school,' he amended grudgingly. 'Do you understand me, gentlemen?'

'Yes, Dad,' two tiny voices chorused. They turned and fled before the wrath of their new father.

Jackie turned apprehensively to her enraged husband and slid appeasing hands over his hard, inflated chest. 'I'm so sorry, Sunny. I never dreamed that they . . .' She faltered to a stop as he suddenly grinned at the retreating backs of two frightened little boys.

Then he looked down at her and began to chuckle. 'Those little monsters are going to get sorted out. Before I'm finished with them they'll be human.' He curved an arm around Jackie's shoulders and winked at her. 'Actually, I've got a terrible confession to make.'

'What is it?' she asked, feeling light-hearted again.

'When I was their age I did the same thing to my dad's car.'

'Oh, Sunny!' she laughed. 'And what did he do to you?'

'The same as they got.'

'Well, you did say that Robert and Edmund needed a father,' she reminded him with a teasing smile.

He growled into his beard. 'They've got that all right.' He started walking her towards the staircase which led to their room. 'Now, Jackie, for their own good, we've got to get started straight away,' he said in his voice of authority.

She looked up at him, completely nonplussed. 'I don't understand. Start what?'

'What our sons need are sisters. Give them a sense of responsibility. Looking after others. It's the only sensible thing to do.' The no-nonsense tone dropped to one of anticipated pleasure. 'A baby girl. I'd be very good with a girl, Jackie.'

'I know you would, Sunny.' Her voice caressed him with her pleasure.

And she was only thirty-one. Young enough to have several girls, if they were blessed with daughters. If they had sons, then Sunny would be to blame, because men determined the sex of any child. Would she tell him? No, not yet. Only if the baby turned out to be a boy. And maybe not even then.

She looked up at him. Sunny would be wonderful with babies. She was sure of that. Sometimes she thought he was still a baby himself, but when they reached the bedroom, she was strongly reminded that he was definitely a very grown-up, very virile and loving man.

Some considerable time later they lay contentedly in each other's arms. Alena's dramatic line in the last Dirk Vescum movie ran through Jackie's mind ... 'Do you think I would want to live without you?' That was precisely how she felt about Sunny. She hugged him more tightly, knowing how precious this man was to her continued happiness. Her love for him tingled through her brain, through her whole body.

Suddenly he propped himself up to look down at her. 'I've decided ... and I won't take no for an answer, Jackie ... that you're to be the musical director for all my movies.'

'But I ... I really don't have the expertise, Sunny.'

'Course you do. You can do anything. Same as myself. In fact, what I'm going to do is make a movie about our relationship. The world is starving for a love-story like ours.'

'But, Sunny ...'

'Hush, woman.' He silenced her with a kiss that was worth being silenced for. When he lifted his head a beatific smile was spreading over his face. 'I have this vision ...'

And who was she to question a vision, Jackie thought, and happily settled herself to listen to the beautifully mad, hopelessly egocentric man that she loved.

Harlequin Presents

Coming Next Month

#1055 PERFECT STRANGERS Amanda Browning
Zoe could hardly believe that Ross's amnesia had robbed him of all memory of her. Yet she dared not defy the doctor's orders not to tell Ross who she was—and what they had once meant to each other.

#1056 NO ESCAPE Daphne Clair
Karen, at eighteen, had fled from her husband and baby, never expecting to see them again. When an unexpected encounter ten years later gave her a second chance, she wondered if she had the courage to accept it....

#1057 A SAVAGE ADORATION Penny Jordan
The humiliation of Dominic's rejection of her adolescent advances had stood between Christy and all other men. Coming home years later, after a career in London, she was dismayed to find Dominic still the one man she desired—and needed.

#1058 BELOVED DECEIVER Flora Kidd
They'd been at university together. Eight years later magazine writer Glenda couldn't understand the changes in Cesar Estrada, now a famous novelist. Why wouldn't he be interviewed, even by her? Did he have something to hide?

#1059 WHIRLWIND Charlotte Lamb
Masking her love for Laird Montgomery was a difficult role for young actress Anna Rendle. But what else could she do? She knew Laird was afraid to return it—for him, love cost too much.

#1060 TO TAME A WOLF Anne McAllister
At least, Jessica thought, two weeks on assignment with Ben in the Michigan woods would prove whether she'd finally got over him—and whether the attraction had been adolescent imagination or something more. She was shocked to realize nothing had changed!

#1061 NIGHT TRAIN Anne Weale
If only she'd never met Carlos Hastings! But she had—and, for Sarah, it was a major decision whether to settle for the secure life of a doctor's wife or risk an affair with charming Carlos, man of the world.

#1062 A LINGERING MELODY Patricia Wilson
Matt had manipulated events to put her back in his power, and Carrie found that the gentle, considerate lover she'd known four years ago had become a hard, unfeeling stranger. He must never know that her twin daughters were his own!

Available in March wherever paperback books are sold, or through Harlequin Reader Service:

In the U.S.
901 Fuhrmann Blvd.
P.O. Box 1397
Buffalo, N.Y. 14240-1397

In Canada
P.O. Box 603
Fort Erie, Ontario
L2A 5X3

Deep in the heart of Africa lay mankind's most awesome secret. Could they find Eden . . . and the grave of Eve?

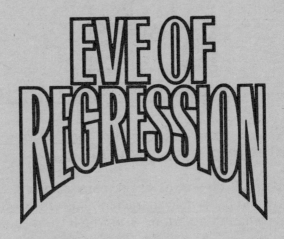

JOHN ARTHUR LONG

A spellbinding novel that combines a fascinating premise with all the ingredients of an edge-of-the-seat read: passion, adventure, suspense and danger.

Available in January at your favorite retail outlet, or reserve your copy for December shipping by sending your name, address, zip or postal code along with a check or money order for $4.70 (includes 75¢ for postage and handling) payable to Worldwide Library to:

<table>
<tr><td><u>In the U.S.</u></td><td><u>In Canada</u></td></tr>
<tr><td>Worldwide Library
901 Fuhrmann Blvd.
Box 1325
Buffalo, NY 14269-1325</td><td>Worldwide Library
P.O. Box 609
Fort Erie, Ontario
L2A 5X3</td></tr>
</table>

Please specify book title with your order.

EVE-1

 ® **WORLDWIDE LIBRARY** ®

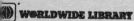